110 Uplifting Short Stories for the Elderly

Heartwarming stories that stimulate the mind and ease tension in elders. Easy-to-read, uplifting and motivational short stories in large print.

SUSANNE B. FLORES

Copyright © 2023 Susanne B. Flores

All rights reserved.

ISBN: 9798396924482

The content contained within this book may not be reproduced, duplicated or transmitted without direct written permission from the author or the publisher.

Legal Notice

This book is copyright protected. This book is only for personal use. You cannot amend, distribute, sell, use, quote or paraphrase any part, or the content within this book, without the consent of the author or publisher.

DEDICATION

This book is lovingly dedicated to all the seniors who continue to embrace life with grace and curiosity, seeking new adventures and opportunities every day.

May these heartwarming tales bring comfort, inspiration, and joy to your lives, just as you have touched so many hearts throughout yours.

Thank you for your unwavering spirit and resilience; may this collection bring you moments of peace and happiness.

Enjoy!

CONTENTS

1 - From Childhood Friends to Soulmates 10
2 - Separated by War, United by Time 11
3 - Building Bridges over Age Divides 12
4 - Rediscovering Creativity through Music 13
5 - Finding Purpose in Community 14
6 - Creating Joyous Memories across Ages 15
7 - A Final Journey: A Tribute to Love 16
8 - Gardening across Generations 17
9 - Embracing Challenges: Seniors' Path to Success 18
10 - The Warmth of Kindness 19
11 - Boston: Resilient City of Champions 20
12 - Ashes Across America 21
13 - A Lifetime of Love and Gardens 23
14 - The artist inside 24
15 - Discovering Creativity Later in Life 26
16 - The Inheritance of Generosity 28
17 - Knit Together: An Unexpected Community 29
18 - Reverse Basketball Revolution 30
19 - The Ageless Spirit of Los Angeles 31
20 - Laugh More Live Longer 33
21 - The Power of Words: A Teacher's Lesson 35
22 - Energetic Age: The Lone Star Line Dancers 36
23 - From History Professor to Eternal Explorer 37
24 - A New Chapter in Paris 38
25 - Beyond expectations: the Surprises of Houston 40
26 - From Catastrophes to Culinary Triumphs 42
27 - Humor on Horseback 43
28 - Adventures with My Cat During Nap Time 44

29 - The Dog Who Brought Laughter Back 45

30 - Houston's Wild Ride 46

31 - The Tower that Saved Dallas 48

32 - The Inheritance of Generosity 50

33 - Unity in the face of war 51

34 - Love Across Generations 52

35 - Finding Joy in Old Age..53

36 - Growing Bolder Not Older 54

37 - Upholding Family Ties Despite Bias 56

38 - Intergenerational Connection Through Art 57

39 - A Philadelphia Story...58

40 - Tim & Clara's San Francisco adventures 60

41 - Making Memories That Last a Lifetime 62

42 - Walter's Bocce Ball Benefits 64

43 - Giggles in the Garden 65

44 - Sand, Sea Breeze, and New Friendships 67

45 - The Garden of Friendship: Evelyn's Story 68

46 - The Beauty of Life: Margaret's Perspective 70

47 - Traditional Tales 72

48 - Secret Letters..73

49 - Once Forbidden 74

50 - Inseparable Shadows..76

51 - Dancing Memories...77

52 - Finding Joy in The Simple Things 78

53 - The Power of Positive Thinking 80

54 - Summer Memories 81

55 - The Power of Positivity 82

56 - The Power of Perseverance: A Sports Story 84

57 - A Helping Hand 85

58 - Memories on Wheels...86

59 - The Ripple Effect of Good Deeds 87

60 - San Francisco: The City That Keeps on Giving 88

61 - Heaven Sent Messenger 90

62 - Frozen Love Flowers 92

63 - Twice Upon a Memory 94

64 - Never Too Late for Love 96

65 - Unbreakable Bonds 97

66 - A Time Before Us 97

67 - From one heart to another 99

68 - Enchanted Moonlight Serenade 100

69 - Wildflowers in Winter 102

70 - Forbidden Melody 103

71 - Two Paths Divided 104

72 - Lost Hearts Unfound 105

73 - New Friends in Old Age 107

74 - Elderly and Animals: A Heartwarming Bond 108

75 - Nature's Uplifting Spirit 109

76 - Snowstorm Tales 110

77 - Love Symphony 112

78 - Embracing the Present Moment with Family 114

79 - Reflections on Nature and Impermanence 115

80 - Whimsical Musings 117

81 - Rebuilding Hope 118

82 - The Unexpected Gift 120

83 - Vintage Car Revival 121

84 - The Power of a Simple Act of Kindness 122

85 - A Second Chance 124

86 - Adversity to Triumph 125

87 - Memories of Youth 126

88 - The Magic Garden 127

89 - Forever Paws: A Story of Love 128

90 - Pets and Purpose: Reflections on Life 129

91 - Max, The Unexpected Joy in Mary's Life 131

92 - Unlikely Friendship: A Heartwarming Story.. 132

93 - A Little Girl's Act of Kindness 133

94 - A Little Kindness Goes a Long Way 134

95 - A Honeymoon to Remember 135

96 - A Story of Old Times 137

97 - The Gift of Time 138

98 - A New Perspective... 139

99 - Innovative Minds: Greatest Inventions 140

100 - Journey of the Heart: Finding Joy in Travel 141

101 - Finding Happiness: A Meadowville Story 142

102 - A Love Woven in Time 144

103 - The Gift of Connection.. 146

104 - Embracing the Power of Compassion 147

105 - A Heartwarming Tale from World War II.. 149

106 - A Bond Beyond Blood: A Tale of Adoption 150

107 - A Heartwarming Tale of Success.. 151

108 - Embracing Joy: A Heartwarming Journey 153

109 - Heartwarming Philanthropy Stories 154

110 - Gratitude's Radiance 156

100 Short Stories for Elderly

1 - From Childhood Friends to Soulmates

Amanda and Mark grew up in neighboring houses and became fast friends before school even entered the equation. But amid all the fun and games of early adolescence came an unforeseeable rift that caused the two to go their separate ways after high school. Little did either know that their adult lives would eventually bring them back together.

The years rolled by until fate arranged a chance meeting one sunny afternoon. While running errands, Amanda stepped into a small boutique and instantly recognized Mark behind the counter, now the owner. As if no time had passed, the floodgates of conversation opened wide between the old companions. Reminiscing, teasing, laughing - every shared moment was familiar, easy, electric. Unbeknownst to either of them, however, this wasn't just platonic camaraderie being rekindled...something else was stirring as well.

Days turned into weeks of catching up, then even longer in each other's company. Intensely drawn to each other despite other romantic attachments, feelings neither ignored nor avoided lingered like persistent spring rain showers. Recognizing the inevitable but unsure whether to risk it all, Amanda confided in her sister (an English teacher) about the situation. Reminiscent of Emily Brontë's tragic lovers in Wuthering Heights, Amanda's sibling recommended that she examine the roots holding up her dear friendship. Once that was done, decisions could follow.

As the trio pored over the details of young Mark and Cathy's doomed affair, the parallels became stark, frighteningly clear. Neither Amanda nor Mark wanted to repeat the mistakes of history or lose forever what made their relationship special. Wisely, they chose to embrace a deeper commitment wholeheartedly rather than settle for half measures.

When they finally joined hands in front of their loved ones and close associates, their vows affirmed a lifelong devotion that honored the passionate intensity that originally bound them.

2 - Separated by War, United by Time

During World War II, Frank was assigned to a field hospital in England, where he worked as a doctor treating wounded soldiers. Amid the chaos of war, Frank met Sarah, a nurse volunteering at the same hospital.

They quickly struck up a close friendship that grew stronger over time. When the fighting ended and the soldiers returned home, Frank and Sarah found themselves separated by continents. Though they wrote letters and phone calls filled the silence, Frank knew deep down that their relationship couldn't last without physical proximity. He didn't know if the universe had a grand plan for him.

After many years had passed, he received a message from a lawyer asking him to fly to New York City urgently. In disbelief, Frank found that Sarah, now retired from nursing, owned a small farm in the country and was anxious for his arrival after seven decades apart.

The emotional reunion took place in her quaint barn under twinkling lights and colorful lanterns strung overhead. And though they never married or had children, they still held hands and enjoyed their twilight years, basking in each other's company and gazing up at the starry sky on crisp summer evenings, living proof that true love finds ways to bind hearts together despite the hardships life throws along the way.

3 - Building Bridges over Age Divides

There was once an elderly woman named Rose who lived alone in a quiet neighborhood. She spent most of her days watching television, reading newspapers, and trying to keep busy. Although she was surrounded by people and families on holidays and weekends, she often felt lonely.

One rainy afternoon, while she was making tea, she heard a knock at her door. To her surprise, it was her neighbor's son, a friendly young boy with whom she rarely interacted. They began to chat and share stories, and soon she realized how much company meant to her. That night, they made plans to spend time together every day after school.

Each day, she would teach him something new and help him with his homework; meanwhile, he would keep her updated with stories from school and share tales of his dreams.

Eventually, through these interactions, they developed an undeniable bond that created countless moments of happiness for both of them. These special connections were nothing short of miraculous to Rose-and reminded her that the beauty of life lies not only in what we accomplish, but also in those with whom we share our journey.

From that point on, whenever she needed something or someone, she knew exactly where to turn for true comfort.

4 - Rediscovering Creativity through Music

There was a woman named Sarah who had always loved music. She had played the piano and sung in choirs throughout her life, but as she grew older, she found herself struggling to find inspiration.

One day, Sarah decided to attend a concert at the local symphony. She was nervous at first, but as she took her seat in the audience, she felt a sense of excitement.

The orchestra began to play, and Sarah was transported to another world. The music was beautiful and powerful, and she felt a sense of joy that she hadn't experienced in years.

After the concert was over, Sarah walked out of the theater feeling inspired. She realized that even though she was getting older, there was still so much beauty in the world.

From that day on, Sarah made a point to attend concerts and musical events whenever she could. She listened to classical music, jazz, and even attended a few rock concerts. She began to play the piano again, and even started a small choir with some of her fellow seniors.

Sarah realized that even though she was getting older, she still had so much to offer the world. She found joy in the simple act of listening to music, and in sharing her love of music with others. And in doing so, she discovered that creativity can flourish at any age.

So if you're ever feeling stuck or uninspired, remember Sarah's story. Take a chance, attend a concert or listen to your favorite album, and see where the music can take you.

5 - Finding Purpose in Community

My dear friend, let me tell you a story that I hope will inspire and motivate you, especially if you enjoy walking.
There was an elderly woman who had always loved to walk. She had spent her life exploring nature, taking long walks through the countryside and along the beach. But as she got older, she found that her physical limitations made it difficult to continue her walking routine.

One day, she heard about a senior walking group in her community. The group met regularly to walk together, exploring different neighborhoods and parks in the area. The woman was hesitant at first, unsure if she could keep up with the group. But she decided to give it a try and was pleasantly surprised by what she found.

The walking group was filled with friendly and welcoming people, all eager to make new friends and enjoy the outdoors together. The woman found that she had a natural rapport with the other members, and she enjoyed their time together immensely. She saw how much the group meant to everyone, and how much joy and sense of community their walks brought.

Over time, the woman's health began to improve. She found that her regular walks with the group gave her a renewed sense of purpose and energy. She began to walk more frequently and even started a program to recruit other older women to join the walking group.

The woman realized that her age and physical limitations didn't have to stop her from pursuing her passion for walking and making new friends. She had found a new way to stay active and engaged in her community, and in the process, she had rediscovered her own sense of purpose and joy.

So, my friend, I encourage you to find ways to stay busy and involved in your community, no matter what your age or physical abilities are. There are always ways to stay in touch and do what you love, like joining a walking group, taking a dance class, or trying a new sport. You never know what relationships and chances will come your way.

6 - Creating Joyous Memories across Ages

There was an elderly woman who had always been passionate about helping others. She had spent her life volunteering for local charities and organizations, but as she grew older, she found that her physical limitations made it difficult to continue her work. She began to feel discouraged and wondered if she would ever be able to make a difference again.

One day, she heard about a program that paired older volunteers with young children who needed extra support and attention. The woman was hesitant at first, unsure if she had the energy and stamina to work with children. But she decided to give it a try and was paired with a young girl who had recently lost her mother.

The woman and the girl began meeting regularly, playing games, reading books, and talking about their lives. The woman found that she had a natural rapport with the girl, and she enjoyed their time together immensely. She saw how much the girl looked up to her and how much their time together meant to her.

Over time, the woman's health began to improve. She found that her work with the girl gave her a renewed sense of purpose and energy. She began volunteering more often and even started a program to recruit other older volunteers to work with children in need.

The woman realized that her age and physical limitations didn't have to stop her from making a difference in the world. She had found a new way to give back and positively impact the lives of others. And in the process, she had rediscovered her own sense of purpose and joy.

So, my friend, I encourage you to seek out opportunities to help others, no matter your age or physical limitations. You never know how much of a difference you can make in someone's life, and in doing so, you may find a renewed sense of purpose and fulfillment in your own life.

7 - A Final Journey: A Tribute to Love

Emma James, a retired schoolteacher, had always lived a quiet and simple life with her beloved husband, John. Together, they traveled beautiful scenic routes across the United States and made countless wonderful memories. But everything changed when John became seriously ill.

After months of battling the disease, John finally succumbed, leaving Emma alone and devastated. With the help of family members, Emma slowly recovered from the ordeal and tried her best to adjust to her new role as a single woman. Eventually, she made a decision: instead of simply accepting her grief, she would embark on a long road trip to scatter John's ashes along her favorite roads and places, honoring his legacy and rekindling her own love of life.

Over the course of several weeks, Emma bravely took to the open road, reliving memories of her past alongside the moments of their shared happiness. In these lonely journeys, she gained strength and confidence, and even opened herself to possible future relationships, finding comfort and guidance in the spirit of her departed lover.

Though tears still flowed frequently, Emma now smiled far more often and cherished every remaining moment as if it were her own.

8 - Gardening across Generations

There was an elderly man who had always been passionate about gardening. He had spent his life cultivating beautiful flowers and plants, and had even won awards for his work. But as he grew older, he found that his physical limitations made it difficult to continue his gardening.

One day, he heard about a program that pairs elderly gardeners with young children who are interested in learning about gardening. The man was hesitant at first, unsure if he had the energy and stamina to work with children. But he decided to give it a try and was paired with a young girl who had never gardened before.

The man and the girl began to meet regularly, planting seeds, weeding, and maintaining the garden. The man found that he had a natural rapport with the girl, and he enjoyed their time together immensely. He saw how much the girl looked up to him and how much their time together meant to her.

Over time, the man's health began to improve. He found that his work with the girl gave him a renewed sense of purpose and energy. He began gardening more often and even started a program to recruit other elderly gardeners to work with children in need.

The man realized that his age and physical limitations didn't have to stop him from pursuing his passion and making a difference in the world. He had found a new way to share his love of gardening and inspire the next generation of gardeners. And in the process, he had rediscovered his own sense of purpose and joy.

So, my friend, I encourage you to seek out opportunities to share your passions and talents with others, no matter your age or physical limitations. You never know how much of a difference you can make in someone's life, and in the process, you may find a renewed sense of purpose and fulfillment in your own.

9 - Embracing Challenges: Seniors' Path to Success

As I sit here on my porch, watching the sun set over the rolling hills of my farm, I can't help but think back on all the seasons that have passed in my life. Like the cycle of nature, my life has had its ups and downs, its successes and failures. But through it all, I have learned important lessons that have made me stronger and wiser.

I remember one particularly difficult season early in my farming career. We suffered heavy losses due to bad weather and poor management decisions. I felt lost and hopeless, unsure if we would make it through another year. But then something changed in me. Instead of feeling defeated, I decided to take a hard look at what wasn't working and what steps I needed to take to make things better.

It was then that I came across the poem "The Road Not Taken" by Robert Frost. Its descriptions of choosing different paths and finding yourself unexpectedly made me rethink my approach. I asked myself what path I should take next, and instead of continuing down the same road of despair, I chose to look for solutions and work toward progress. Over time, we turned our fortunes around and eventually prospered because I allowed myself to change course when necessary and not stubbornly cling to old ways.

Today, as fall approaches and the leaves begin to change color again, I am reminded that growth is indeed a cyclical process. Sometimes we flourish, sometimes we falter, but each experience offers us opportunities to learn, to grow, and ultimately to thrive in the face of challenges. And just as Robert Frost did for me, I hope my reflections will inspire other seniors facing difficult moments and show them the power of perseverance and adaptability, no matter your age.

10 - The Warmth of Kindness

There was an elderly man who had always had a passion for helping others. He had spent his life volunteering with local charities and organizations, but as he grew older, he found that his physical limitations made it difficult to continue his work. He began to feel discouraged and wondered if he would ever be able to make a difference again.

One day, he heard about a program that paired older volunteers with young children who needed extra support and attention. The man was hesitant at first, unsure if he had the energy and stamina to work with children. But he decided to give it a try and was paired with a young boy who had recently lost his father.

The man and the boy began to meet regularly, playing games, reading books, and talking about their lives. The man found that he had a natural rapport with the boy, and he enjoyed their time together immensely. He saw how much the boy looked up to him and how much their time together meant to him.

Over time, the man's health began to improve. He found that his work with the boy gave him a renewed sense of purpose and energy. He began volunteering more often and even started a program to recruit other older volunteers to work with children in need.

The man realized that his age and physical limitations didn't have to stop him from making a difference in the world. He had found a new way to give back and positively impact the lives of others. And in the process, he had rediscovered his own sense of purpose and joy.

So, my friend, I encourage you to seek out opportunities to help others, regardless of your age or physical limitations. You never know how much of a difference you can make in someone's life, and in doing so, you may find a renewed sense of purpose and fulfillment in your own life.

11 - Boston: Resilient City of Champions

Boston, the City of Champions, has a rich history and vibrant culture that has inspired countless people throughout the years. From the cobblestone streets of

Beacon Hill to the bustling waterfront of the Seaport District, Boston is a city full of life and energy.

One of the most inspiring things about Boston is its resilience. The city has faced its fair share of challenges over the years, from the devastating Boston Marathon bombing to harsh winters that can bring the city to a standstill. But through it all, Bostonians have shown an unwavering spirit and a determination to overcome any obstacle.

This resilience was on full display during the COVID-19 pandemic. As the city was hit hard by the virus, Bostonians came together to support each other. They donated food and supplies to those in need, and they found creative ways to stay connected even when they couldn't be together in person.

One of the most inspiring examples was the way Boston's musicians came together to lift people's spirits during the pandemic. From virtual concerts to impromptu performances on porches and street corners, Boston's musicians found ways to share their talents and bring joy to others.

As the city begins to emerge from the pandemic, Bostonians are once again demonstrating their resilience. They are coming together to support local businesses, celebrate the city's rich history and culture, and look forward to a brighter future.

Boston may be a city of champions, but it is also a city of survivors. Through its challenges and triumphs, Boston has proven to be a place of hope and inspiration, a place where anything is possible.

12 - Ashes Across America

Mrs. Emma James had retired from teaching after a long and fulfilling career. But her life had taken a sad turn after the death of her beloved husband, John. John had always loved adventure and travel, and they had enjoyed many scenic routes together over the years. Now, Emma decided to take a road trip to scatter John's cremated remains along the same scenic routes they had enjoyed together.

As Emma packed for the trip, she found old photos, keepsakes, and journals that reminded her of their life together. She felt a pang of sadness as she remembered the good times they had shared, but also a sense of gratitude for the memories they had created.

Emma began her journey, driving along winding roads, through mountains and valleys, and across picturesque landscapes. Along the way, she stopped at scenic overlooks to breathe in the fresh air and take in the beauty around her. As she scattered John's ashes, she felt a sense of peace and closure, knowing that he was finally at rest in the places he loved so much.

But the journey was not just about scattering John's ashes. It was also a journey of rediscovery, as Emma found old photos and journals that brought back warm memories of their life together. She remembered the day they first met, at a college dance, and the way John had swept her off her feet. She remembered how he had proposed to her on a hot air balloon ride over the countryside, and how they had laughed and cried together over the years.

As Emma read through John's journals, she saw how much he had loved her and how much he had cherished their life together. He had written about their travels, their adventures, and how they had grown old together, but never stopped exploring the world around them.

Emma's journey also brought her face to face with the reality of mortality. She realized that life was fleeting and that the time she had left was precious. She thought about all the things she still wanted to do, the places she still wanted to see, and the people she still wanted to meet.

As she drove on, Emma began to see the world in a new light. She saw the beauty of life, even in its impermanence. She saw how the world continued to change and evolve, and how people continued to love and cherish each other even after death.
When Emma finally finished her journey, she felt a sense of peace and contentment. She knew that John's spirit would always be with her, guiding her and inspiring her to continue exploring the world around her. She also knew that her journey had been about more than just scattering his ashes. It was about rediscovering the love they had shared and the beauty of life, even in its impermanence.

As Emma drove home, she felt a renewed sense of purpose. She knew that her journey had not only been about saying goodbye to John, but also about rediscovering herself and the world around her. She vowed to keep exploring, to keep learning, and to keep loving, just as John had taught her.
In the end, Emma's journey had been one of emotional exploration, echoing Mary Shelley's exploration of relationships and mortality in Frankenstein. But unlike Shelley's tragic tale, Emma's journey had been one of hope and renewal, reminding her that love and adventure were still possible, even in the face of mortality.

13 - A Lifetime of Love and Gardens

In his golden years, Henry often visited the local botanical garden with his wife, Jane. It became a sacred place for both of them, filled with fond memories of their youthful love affair. The couple met during a flower arranging class at the community center and soon discovered that they shared not only an interest in plants, but also a deep affection for each other. Throughout their marriage, they continued to cultivate beauty in the natural world around them, finding solace in its simplicity and grace.

Today, standing among the vibrant flora and fauna, Henry recalls his lifelong journey with Jane. He remembers how they used gardens as a language to communicate their feelings; they planted a rosebush for each year of their union, each representing a milestone or triumph. They even created a secret corner of blue forget-me-nots as a nod to Shakespeare's Juliet, a quiet reminder of their undying devotion. Now these same flowers serve as a poignant symbol of Jane's absence, yet Henry finds comfort in knowing that she is still entwined within him.

Henry smiles wistfully as he reflects on the richness of a partnership built on mutual admiration and respect. From traveling throughout Europe, exploring the cultural landmarks associated with the great Romantic poets, to building a cozy nest with their beloved pets, Henry and Jane have relished the adventure of life together. Their unwavering faith in each other helped them weather the trials of time, allowing them to grow stronger and deeper as soul mates.

His thoughts drift to Gerard Manley Hopkins, whose poetry captured the essence of the natural world with its intricate details. The lines of "Spring and Fall," which resonate deeply with Henry, evoke the fleeting nature of existence, yet hint at the ability of eternal love to transcend mortality. Leaves like the things of men, you

With your fresh thoughts, can you provide an inventory of all the world's freshest materials, as well as some of those in season? We have them in abundance here. But we call them 'spare.

14 - The artist inside

Maggie had always loved art, but she had never felt she had any real talent for it. As a young woman, she had taken a few classes here and there, but life had gotten in the way. She had married, had children, and spent most of her working years as a nurse. Now, at age 84 and living in a retirement home, Maggie had all the time in the world, but she still didn't feel like she had anything to do.

One day, her nurse suggested she try the art therapy program the home offered. Maggie was reluctant at first, but finally agreed to give it a try. On the day of the class, she shuffled into the small art room, unsure of what to expect.

The art therapist, a young woman named Emily, greeted her warmly and led her to a seat at a large table. There were already a few other residents there, all with different levels of experience and skills. Maggie felt a little intimidated at first, but Emily quickly put her at ease.
Emily started the class by leading everyone through some relaxation exercises. Maggie had never really done anything like this before, but she found that she enjoyed it. She closed her eyes and focused on her breathing, letting go of all the worries and stress that had been weighing on her.

After the relaxation exercises, Emily passed out some paper and watercolors. She told everyone to just start painting without worrying about what they were making or whether it looked good or not. Maggie dipped her brush into the paint and began to make some tentative strokes on the paper.

As she worked, a strange thing began to happen. Maggie found that she lost track of time and she felt as if she was completely immersed in what she was doing. She forgot all her aches and pains, her worries and regrets. She was just focused on the colors and shapes on the page in front of her.

Before she knew it, the lesson was over. Emily asked everyone to show their work, and Maggie felt a little self-conscious. But when she saw what the others had made, she realized that it didn't matter. Everyone had created something unique and beautiful.

Over the next few weeks, Maggie went to the art therapy class every week. She started experimenting with different materials and techniques and found that she was enjoying it more and more. She began to look forward to the class each week, and she felt that it gave her something to look forward to.

One day, Emily asked Maggie if she would be interested in participating in an art show that the shelter was having. Maggie was reluctant at first, but Emily encouraged her. She told her that she had real talent and that people would love to see her work.

With a little encouragement, Maggie agreed. She spent the next few weeks working on a painting that she was proud of. It was a colorful abstract with swirls of blue, green, and yellow. When the day of the art show came, Maggie was nervous but excited.

The show was a great success. Maggie's painting was one of the most popular pieces there, and she received many compliments. She felt a sense of pride that she hadn't felt in a long time, and she realized that she had found something that gave her a sense of purpose.

As she walked back to her room that night, Maggie felt as if a weight had been lifted from her shoulders. She realized that it didn't matter that she had never taken art seriously before. All that mattered was that she was doing it now and that it made her happy.

15 - Discovering Creativity Later in Life

Art has the power to inspire and transform people of all ages, but it can be especially meaningful for older adults. As we age, we may face physical limitations or health challenges that make it difficult to engage in the activities we once enjoyed. But art can provide a sense of purpose and fulfillment that transcends these limitations.

I remember working with a group of older adults at a local community center. Many of them had never considered themselves artists, but as we began to explore different media and techniques, they discovered a newfound passion for creativity.

One woman in particular stands out in my mind. She was in her late 80's and had recently lost her husband of over 60 years. She was struggling with grief and loneliness and had lost much of her sense of purpose and joy in life.

But as she began to experiment with painting and drawing, I could see a transformation taking place. She began to express her feelings and memories through her art, creating beautiful and poignant works that spoke to the depth of her experience.

Over time, she began to share her art with others, showing her paintings at local galleries and community events. She even began teaching art classes to other seniors, sharing her newfound passion and inspiring others to explore their own creativity.

Through art, this woman had found a new sense of purpose and meaning in life. She had found a way to connect with others and express herself in a way that transcended words or physical limitations.

And she was not alone. I've seen countless examples of older people finding new joy and purpose through art, whether it's painting, sculpture, photography, or any other medium.

So if you ever find yourself feeling disconnected or lost, I encourage you to explore the world of art. Whether you're an experienced artist or a complete beginner, there's always something new to discover and explore. And who knows? You might just find a new passion that will change your life in ways you never thought possible.

16 - The Inheritance of Generosity

Edith was a kind-hearted woman who lived alone in a small apartment near London Bridge. She had always struggled financially, but she never let poverty harden her soul. Whenever someone needed help, she helped in any way she could. But after retirement, Edith found herself struggling even more. She couldn't keep up with her rent payments and was facing eviction from her home. Edith was truly living paycheck to paycheck.

One morning, Edith received an envelope containing a letter and a check. Perplexed, she carefully opened it and read the contents. To her surprise, she was informed that a distant relative had left her a substantial inheritance. At first, she thought it must be a mistake or a scam. But upon further investigation, she realized that the gift was genuine and would allow her to live comfortably for the rest of her days.

Edith was torn - part of her wanted to leave London, buy a cottage somewhere in the country, and enjoy her golden years away from the noise and crowds of city life. Another part, the better angel of her nature, urged her to use her windfall to help others less fortunate. Deciding to split the difference, she bought a smaller apartment closer to the river and donated a portion of her inheritance to several nearby charities. A generous benefactor, Edith quietly worked miracles for those in need.

Word of her good deeds quickly spread throughout the neighborhood. People approached her for help, confident that she wouldn't turn anyone away. Edith listened compassionately and offered whatever assistance she could. In the process, her own burdens seemed to lighten. True wealth lay not in material possessions, but in the human connections that were nurtured and maintained. Like characters in Elizabeth Gaskell or Anthony Trollope, Edith understood the importance of community and giving freely. And like them, she was treasured for it.

In the remaining years of her long life, Edith embraced philanthropy, ensuring that many found warmth on cold winter nights and hot meals when hunger gnawed at empty bellies. Ultimately, her legacy inspired similar acts of selflessness among friends, neighbors, and strangers alike, transforming the once rough-and-tumble neighborhood into a thriving, caring community characterized by kindness rather than indifference or greed. Despite her frail body, Edith left behind an enduring spirit of hope, love, and generosity that permeated the very air of Old London.

17 - Knit Together: An Unexpected Community

In a cozy little town, there lived an elderly woman named Clara. She had lived in the town all her life, and as she grew older, she felt increasingly lonely. Most of her friends had either moved away or died, and her children were busy with their own lives.

One day, Clara decided to visit the town's community center, hoping to find a new activity to fill her days. As she walked through the center, she noticed a group of people gathered around a table, laughing and talking. Curious, she approached the group and discovered that they were participating in a weekly knitting club.

The leader of the club, a warm and friendly woman named Rose, noticed Clara's interest and invited her to join the group. Clara was hesitant at first because she hadn't knitted in years and was unsure of her skills. But Rose's kind words and the welcoming smiles of the other members convinced her to give it a try.

As Clara picked up her needles and began to make her first scarf, she found herself immersed in the soothing rhythm of the stitches and the camaraderie of the group. The other members, who ranged in age, shared their own knitting tips and stories, and Clara felt a sense of belonging that she hadn't experienced in a long time.

Over the next few weeks, Clara continued to attend the knitting club and found that her loneliness began to fade. She formed close friendships with the other members and discovered a newfound passion for knitting. The scarves, hats, and blankets she created brought warmth not only to her home, but also to her heart.

In the end, Clara learned that it's never too late to find new friends and happiness in unexpected places. The knitting club not only filled her days with joy, but also gave her a sense of purpose and community that she had been missing for years.

18 - Reverse Basketball Revolution

Once upon a time, there was a high school basketball team that had never won a game. They were the laughingstock of the league, and their opponents often joked about how easy it was to beat them. But despite their losing record, the team never gave up.

One day, the coach decided to try a new strategy. He gathered the team and told them they were going to play a game of "reverse basketball. The rules were simple: the team that scored the fewest points would win.

At first, the players were confused. They had never heard of it before. But the coach explained that it was a way to take the pressure off and have some fun. The team agreed to try it.

The game started, and the players quickly realized that this was going to be a lot harder than they thought. They were so used to trying to score that they didn't know how to play defense. But as the game went on, they started to get the hang of it.

The crowd was in hysterics as they watched the two teams struggle to score. But the high school team was determined to win, even if it meant scoring less than their opponents. They played with a newfound energy and enthusiasm, and before they knew it, the game was over.
The final score was 2-1 in favor of the high school team.

They had won their first game, even though it was a reverse basketball game. The players were ecstatic, and the crowd cheered them on as they celebrated their victory.

From that day on, the high school team played with a new sense of confidence and determination. They still lost some games, but they never gave up. And every time they stepped on the court, they remembered the game of reverse basketball and the joy and laughter it brought them. They knew that no matter what, they could always find a way to have fun and enjoy the game they loved.

19 - The Ageless Spirit of Los Angeles

Los Angeles, the City of Angels, is known for its sunny weather, palm trees, and bustling entertainment industry. For an elderly man named Jack, it had been home for more than 40 years. He had seen the city change and grow, but his love for Los Angeles remained strong.
One day, Jack's grandson, Alex, came to visit and noticed that his grandfather seemed a bit down. When asked what was bothering him, Jack sighed and said, "I just feel like I'm getting too old for this town. Things are changing so fast, and I can't keep up.

Alex knew his grandfather needed a change of pace, so he decided to take him on a bike ride around Los Angeles to show him a different side of the city. They started with a ride along the famous Venice Beach Boardwalk, where they enjoyed the ocean breeze and lively atmosphere. Jack was amazed by the energy of the place and felt a renewed sense of excitement.
Next, they rode their bikes to the Griffith Observatory, where they marveled at the breathtaking view of the city

and the stars above. Jack had always been fascinated by astronomy, but he had never visited the observatory. He was captivated by the beauty of the cosmos and felt a renewed sense of wonder.

As they pedaled through the city, Alex pointed out all the little things that made Los Angeles special. They stopped at a food truck for some delicious tacos, and Jack laughed as he tried to eat his meal without spilling salsa on his shirt. They rode their bikes along the LA River Bike Path, enjoying the unique urban landscape.

They eventually arrived in downtown Los Angeles, where they explored historic Olvera Street and Union Station. The vibrant culture and history of the area made Jack feel like he was in another world. As they rode their bikes back to Jack's house, he turned to Alex and said, "You know, I never realized how much I love this city until today. Thank you for showing me another side of it.

From that day on, Jack began to see Los Angeles in a new light. He took walks in his neighborhood, visited museums, and explored different parts of the city. He even joined a local senior cycling club, something he had always wanted to do but never had the time.

As he became more involved in the community, Jack made new friends and discovered that there was a world of opportunity waiting for him in Los Angeles. He volunteered at a local food bank and began attending events at a nearby community center, feeling like he was making a difference in the world.

The years passed and Jack grew older, but he never lost his love for Los Angeles. Even when he could no longer ride his bike as easily as he used to, he would sit on his porch and watch the city go by, grateful for all the memories he had made there.

And whenever Alex came to visit, they would rent bikes or explore a new part of town, and Jack would tell him stories about the Los Angeles he loved. He knew that no matter what happened, Los Angeles would always have a special place in his heart.

20 - Laugh More Live Longer

In the bustling city of Washington, D.C., a group of lively senior citizens decided to form a unique club called the Golden Age Pranksters. Their mission was simple: to spread joy and laughter throughout the city by pulling light-hearted pranks and sharing their wisdom with a touch of humor.

The group was led by a charismatic 75-year-old named Walter, who had a twinkle in his eye and an infectious laugh. A retired history teacher, Walter loved to regale his fellow pranksters with tales of the city's past, always with a humorous twist.

One sunny afternoon, the Golden Age Pranksters gathered on the National Mall, armed with a plan to bring smiles to the faces of tourists and locals alike. They set up a booth offering "free advice from wise elders," and soon people were lining up, curious to hear what these spirited seniors had to say.

A young couple approached the booth seeking advice on how to maintain a happy marriage. Walter leaned over and said, "Always remember that a successful marriage is like a good pot of soup-it takes time, patience, and a good sense of humor to get it just right. The couple laughed and thanked Walter for his wisdom.

Next, a harried businessman asked for tips on dealing with stress. Another comedian, 80-year-old Betty, replied, "Take a deep breath, count to ten, and remember - you can't control everything, but you can control how you react to it. And don't forget to laugh!" The businessman smiled and felt a weight lifted from his shoulders.

As the day wore on, the Golden Age Pranksters continued to share their wit and wisdom, leaving a trail of laughter in their wake. They even managed to sneak in a few harmless pranks, like placing whoopee cushions on park benches and handing out fortune cookies with funny messages inside.

The Golden Age Pranksters proved that age is just a number and that laughter really is the best medicine. Their uplifting spirit and playful antics brought joy to the city of Washington and reminded everyone that life is better when you embrace your inner prankster and face each day with a smile.

21 - The Power of Words: A Teacher's Lesson

Once upon a time, there was a man named Jack who had lived his entire life with a passion for music. He was an excellent pianist and had always dreamed of performing in front of a large audience. However, Jack was born with a severe hearing impairment that made pursuing his dream nearly impossible.

Despite his disability, Jack refused to give up on his passion. He spent countless hours practicing, memorizing the vibrations of every note and chord in his body. Even though he could not hear the music with his ears, he felt it with his heart and soul.

One day, Jack heard about a concert for people with disabilities being organized by a local community center. He saw this as an opportunity to share his music with the world. Without hesitation, he signed up to perform.

The night of the concert, the auditorium was packed with people of all ages and abilities. Jack sat nervously at the piano, his heart pounding with excitement and anticipation. As he began to play, he closed his eyes and let the music flow through him. The notes came alive in his fingers, dancing across the keys in a symphony of sound.

The audience was stunned. They had never heard music like this - so raw, so passionate, so full of life. Jack's disability had been turned into a gift, allowing him to create music that was more beautiful and moving than anything they had ever heard.

After the concert, people came up to Jack with tears in their eyes and told him how his music had touched their hearts. They told him that he had given them hope, that he had inspired them to never give up on their dreams.

From that day on, Jack's music became known around the world. He continued to perform with passion and determination, inspiring others to find their own unique gifts and talents and never let their disabilities hold them back.

22 - Energetic Age: The Lone Star Line Dancers

In the heart of Texas, a group of spirited seniors formed an unconventional club called the Lone Star Line Dancers. Their goal was simple: to spread happiness and energy throughout the state by showcasing their impressive line dancing skills and proving that age is no barrier to having fun.

The group was led by a vivacious 72-year-old named Daisy, who had a knack for making people laugh and a passion for dancing. Daisy was a retired dance instructor, and she loved teaching her fellow seniors new moves while sharing amusing anecdotes from her dancing days.

One warm evening, the Lone Star Line Dancers decided to surprise the patrons of a local barbecue joint with an impromptu performance. As the sun began to set, the seniors took their positions and began dancing to the lively tunes of a nearby country band.

The crowd couldn't help but smile as they watched the energetic seniors twirl, stomp, and clap in perfect unison. Daisy led the group with a beaming smile, her cowboy hat bobbing in time to the music. The audience quickly joined in, clapping and cheering for the talented dancers.

After their performance, the Lone Star Line Dancers mingled with the crowd, sharing stories and laughter with people of all ages. One young woman approached Daisy and asked for advice on how to stay active as she got older. Daisy winked and replied, "Honey, just keep dancing and laughing and you'll stay young at heart forever.

As the night wore on, the seniors continued to dance and share their joy with everyone around them. Their infectious energy and zest for life inspired others to join in, transforming the barbecue joint into a lively dance party under the Texas stars.

The Lone Star Line Dancers proved that age is just a state of mind and that laughter and dancing can bring people together, no matter their age. Their uplifting spirit and lively performances brought happiness to the people of Texas and reminded everyone that life is best enjoyed with a little humor and a lot of dancing.

23 - From History Professor to Eternal Explorer

In the enchanting city of Rome, a group of senior citizens came together to form a unique club called the Eternal City Explorers. Their mission was to rediscover the beauty and history of Rome while sharing their wisdom and enthusiasm with others, proving that age is no barrier to adventure.

The group was led by a charming 70-year-old named Giovanni, a retired history professor with a passion for storytelling. Giovanni loved to share fascinating tales of Rome's past with his fellow explorers, always adding a touch of humor and wit to keep everyone entertained.

One sunny morning, the Eternal City Explorers set out to discover Rome's lesser-known gems. Armed with maps and curiosity, they navigated the winding cobblestone streets, stopping to admire hidden courtyards and ancient fountains.

As they explored, the seniors struck up conversations with locals and tourists alike, sharing their knowledge of Rome's history and offering friendly advice on the best places to visit. One young couple, captivated by Giovanni's stories, asked him his secret for staying so energetic and engaged in his golden years. He smiled and replied, "Keep learning, stay curious, and never lose your sense of wonder.

The Eternal City Explorers continued their journey, visiting charming cafes, bustling markets, and serene parks. Along the way, they collected stories, laughter, and new friendships, leaving a trail of inspiration in their wake.

As the sun began to set, the group gathered in a picturesque piazza to share their discoveries and reminisce about the day's adventures. They toasted to the eternal beauty of Rome and the timeless joy of exploration.

The Eternal City Explorers demonstrated that age is just a number and that curiosity and a sense of adventure can keep the spirit young. Their uplifting journey through Rome reminded everyone they met that life is best lived with an open heart, a curious mind, and a willingness to embrace the unknown.

24 - A New Chapter in Paris

In the heart of Paris, there is a small café tucked away on a quiet street. It is a place where locals gather to share stories, sip coffee, and watch the world go by. One day, an elderly woman named Marie stumbled upon this café. She had lived in Paris all her life, but had never ventured into this part of the city. As she sat down at a table, she couldn't help but feel a sense of excitement and curiosity. What other hidden gems had she yet to discover in her beloved city?

As she sipped her coffee, Marie struck up a conversation with the owner of the café, a kind and wise man named Jean. They talked about life, love, and the beauty of Paris. Jean told Marie his own story of how he had come to open the café and how it had become a haven for those seeking a moment of peace and tranquility in the bustling city.

Marie left the café that day feeling invigorated and inspired. She realized that even though she had lived in

Paris for so long, there was still so much to discover and explore. She made a promise to herself to seek out new experiences and adventures, no matter how big or small.

Over the next few weeks, Marie began to explore Paris with a newfound sense of wonder and curiosity. She visited museums and galleries she had never been to before, tried new foods and wines, and even took a dance class. She met new people, made new friends, and felt more alive than she had in years.

As she sat in the cafe one day, reflecting on her recent adventures, Marie realized something important. She had always thought that her age was a barrier to trying new things and experiencing new joys. But in reality, it was her own mindset that was holding her back. She had been so focused on what she couldn't do that she had forgotten all the things she could do.

From that day on, Marie made a conscious effort to embrace life with open arms. She continued to explore Paris and all its wonders, but also began volunteering at a local charity and taking up a new hobby. She realized that age was just a number and that there was no limit to what she could accomplish if she set her mind to it.

As Marie sat in the café, surrounded by the warmth and love of her newfound community, she felt a deep sense of gratitude. She was grateful for the beauty of Paris, for the kindness of strangers, and for the endless possibilities that life had to offer. She knew that whatever challenges lay ahead, she would face them with courage and determination, just as she had faced the challenge of rediscovering herself in the heart of Paris.

I hope this story has inspired you to embrace life with open arms, no matter your age or circumstances. Remember that there is always something new to discover and that the beauty of life is in the journey, not just the destination. May you find joy, love, and adventure in all your days, just as Marie did in the heart of Paris.

25 - Beyond expectations: the Surprises of Houston

One day, an elderly man named George was visiting Houston for the first time. He had always been curious about the city, with its towering skyscrapers and bustling energy. As he walked down the street, he couldn't help but feel a sense of excitement and wonder.

As he admired the architecture of a particularly impressive building, he suddenly heard a loud noise behind him. He turned to see a group of cowboys riding down the street on horseback, yelling and screaming as they went.

George was taken aback by the sight, but couldn't help but laugh at the absurdity of it all. He had never seen anything like it in his life. As the cowboys rode off into the distance, George continued on his way, feeling more energetic and alive than he had in years.
Later that day, George visited the Johnson Space Center, where he marveled at the incredible achievements of the astronauts who had explored the cosmos. He even met a real astronaut who regaled him with stories of space travel and adventure.

As he was leaving the space center, George suddenly heard another loud noise. This time it was a group of oil drillers celebrating a successful well. They were covered in oil and dirt, but they were grinning from ear to ear.

George couldn't help but laugh at the sight. He had never

seen such a motley crew in one place. But he also realized something important. Houston was a city of contrasts, where cowboys and astronauts, oil drillers and scientists coexisted in harmony.

As George continued to explore Houston, he encountered more and more funny and inspiring moments. He saw a group of street performers put on a hilarious comedy show and even got to sample some delicious Tex-Mex cuisine.

By the end of his trip, George realized that Houston was a city that embodied the spirit of adventure and possibility. It was a place where anything could happen, and where people from all walks of life could come together to create something truly special.

As he boarded his plane back home, George felt a sense of gratitude for the experiences he had had in Houston. He knew that he would never forget the cowboys, the astronauts, and the oil drillers who had made his trip so memorable.

And so, my dear friend, I hope that this funny story has inspired you to embrace life with a sense of humor and adventure, no matter your age or circumstance. Remember that laughter is the best medicine, and that there is always something new and exciting to discover, even in a city as familiar as Houston. May you find joy, laughter, and inspiration in all your days, just as George did in the heart of Houston.

26 - From Catastrophes to Culinary Triumphs

Cooking can be a fulfilling activity, but it can also be a source of frustration and humor. One day, an elderly woman named Margaret decided to try a new recipe she had found in a cookbook. She was excited to try something new and delicious, but little did she know that her cooking adventure would turn out to be quite comical.

As she began to gather the ingredients, Margaret realized that she was missing a few key ingredients. Undaunted, she decided to improvise and use what she had on hand. She substituted butter for oil and used a different type of cheese than the recipe called for.

As she began to mix the ingredients, Margaret realized that the dough was much thicker than it should be. She tried to thin it with some milk, but it only made things worse. The dough became lumpy and unmanageable, and Margaret began to feel frustrated.

Just as she was about to give up, her granddaughter came into the kitchen. She took one look at the mess on the counter and burst out laughing. Margaret couldn't help but join in, and soon they were both giggling uncontrollably.
Together they decided to salvage what they could of the dough and make something new. They added some extra spices and herbs and baked the mixture in a muffin tin. To their surprise, the result was delicious! The muffins were savory and flavorful, with a crisp crust and a soft, fluffy interior.

As they sat down to enjoy their creation, Margaret realized something important. Cooking wasn't just about following a recipe or doing everything perfectly. It was about having fun, being creative, and enjoying the process. She had learned that sometimes the best things in life come from unexpected twists and turns.

And so, my dear older friend, I hope this funny story has inspired you to embrace the joy and humor of cooking.

Remember that it's okay to make mistakes and improvise, and that sometimes the best recipes come from unexpected combinations. May you find laughter, creativity, and deliciousness in all your culinary adventures.

27 - Humor on Horseback

Horses are majestic creatures that have captured the hearts of many, but they can also be a source of humor and laughter. One day, an elderly man named John decided to take a riding lesson. He had always been fascinated by horses and was excited to finally learn how to ride one.

As he mounted the horse, John felt a sense of exhilaration and freedom. He was finally living his childhood dream of being a cowboy. But as the lesson began, things quickly took a comical turn.

The horse, it seemed, had a mind of its own. It refused to follow John's commands and instead began trotting in circles around the arena. John tried to stay calm and focused, but he couldn't help but feel a little silly.

Just as he was about to give up, the horse suddenly stopped. John looked down and saw that the horse had spotted a patch of grass on the ground and was happily munching on it.

John couldn't help but laugh at the sight. Here he was, trying to learn to ride a horse, and the horse was more interested in eating grass. But as he watched the horse, he realized something important. Sometimes it's okay to slow down and enjoy the simple things in life.

Together, John and the horse spent the rest of the lesson

walking around the arena, stopping to smell the flowers and enjoy the sunshine. It wasn't the lesson John was expecting, but it was exactly what he needed.

As he dismounted, John felt a sense of gratitude and joy. He had learned that sometimes the best moments in life come from unexpected twists and turns. And he had also learned that horses, like people, have their own personalities and quirks.

Remember that sometimes the best moments come from unexpected places, and that it's okay to slow down and enjoy the simple things. May you find laughter, joy, and unexpected adventures in all your days, just as John did on the back of a horse.

28 - Adventures with My Cat During Nap Time

Cats are fascinating creatures that have been the subject of many funny stories and jokes. One day, an elderly woman named Alice was sitting in her garden, enjoying the sunshine and flowers. Suddenly, she heard a loud meowing sound coming from the bushes.

As she approached the bushes, she saw a small kitten mewing pitifully. Alice couldn't resist the kitten's adorable face and decided to take it in as her own.

But as she soon discovered, the kitten had a mischievous streak. It loved to play with balls of yarn, knock over vases, and climb up curtains. Alice found herself constantly chasing after the kitten, trying to keep it out of trouble.

One day, Alice came home to find that the kitten had climbed up the kitchen counter and was now perched on top of the refrigerator. Alice couldn't help but laugh at the sight. Here was a tiny kitten acting like it owned the place.

As she reached up to grab the kitten, it suddenly jumped down on her head. Alice couldn't help but laugh even harder. She had not felt so alive and playful in years.

From that day on, Alice and the kitten became inseparable. They spent their days playing, sleeping, and exploring the world around them. Alice realized that the kitten had brought a sense of joy and humor to her life that had long been missing.

And so, my dear older friend, I hope this funny story has inspired you to embrace the humor and joy of life, no matter your age or circumstances. Remember that sometimes the best things in life come from unexpected sources, and that it's okay to be playful and silly. May you find laughter, joy, and unexpected adventures in all your days, just as Alice did with her mischievous kitten.

29 - The Dog Who Brought Laughter Back

One day, an elderly man named Tom was walking his dog, Max, in the park. Max was a friendly and energetic dog, always eager to meet new people and make new friends.

As they walked, Max suddenly spotted a squirrel and took off after it, dragging Tom behind him. Tom couldn't help but laugh at the sight. Here he was, being dragged along by a dog half his size.

As they continued their walk, Max began to sniff around a nearby tree. Tom assumed that Max was just doing his business, but to his surprise, Max suddenly started digging furiously at the base of the tree.

Tom couldn't help but laugh at the sight. Here was a dog digging like his life depended on it, all for the sake of a buried bone.

As they continued their walk, Tom realized something important. Max had brought a sense of joy and humor to his life that had been missing for a long time. He had not felt so alive and playful in years.

From that day on, Tom and Max became inseparable. They spent their days playing fetch, going for walks, and exploring the world around them. Tom realized that Max had brought a sense of purpose and companionship to his life that he had long been missing.

And so, my dear older friend, I hope this funny story has inspired you to embrace the humor and joy of life. May you find laughter, joy, and unexpected adventures in all your days, just as Tom did with his faithful companion, Max.

30 - Houston's Wild Ride

Houston is a city known for its diversity, energy and sense of humor. One day, an elderly man named Frank was visiting Houston for the first time. He had always been curious about the city, with its towering skyscrapers and bustling energy. As he walked down the street, he couldn't help but feel a sense of excitement and wonder.

As he admired the architecture of a particularly impressive building, he suddenly heard a loud noise behind him. He turned to see a group of cowboys riding down the street on horseback, yelling and screaming as they went.

Frank was taken aback by the sight, but couldn't help but laugh at the absurdity of it all. He had never seen anything like it in his life. As the cowboys rode off into the distance, Frank continued on his way, feeling more energetic and alive than he had in years.

Later that day, Frank visited Space Center Houston, where he marveled at the incredible achievements of the astronauts who had explored the cosmos. He even met a real astronaut who regaled him with stories of space travel and adventure.

As he was leaving the space center, Frank suddenly heard another loud noise. This time it was a group of oil drillers celebrating a successful well. They were covered in oil and dirt, but they were grinning from ear to ear.

Frank couldn't help but laugh at the sight. He had never seen such a motley crew in one place. But he also realized something important. Houston was a city of contrasts, where cowboys and astronauts, oil drillers and scientists coexisted in harmony.

As Frank continued to explore Houston, he encountered more and more funny and inspiring moments. He saw a group of street performers put on a hilarious comedy show and even got to sample some delicious Tex-Mex cuisine.
By the end of his trip, Frank realized that Houston was a city that embodied the spirit of adventure and possibility. It was a place where anything could happen, and where people from all walks of life could come together to create something truly special.

As he boarded his plane back home, Frank felt a sense of gratitude for his experiences in Houston. He knew he would never forget the cowboys, astronauts and oil drillers who had made his trip so memorable.

31 - The Tower that Saved Dallas

As an artist, I have always been interested in how music can motivate and lift the spirits of people of all ages. But it was not until I started working with the elderly that I really began to understand how music can change people.

I remember the first time I played my guitar for a group of elderly people at a local nursing home. At first they seemed hesitant and shy, as if they did not know what to make of this young artist. But when I started playing some old folk songs on the guitar, I could see their faces light up with recognition and happiness.

One woman in particular interested me. She was sitting in the back of the room with her eyes closed and a small smile on her lips. As I played, she began to gently dance to the beat of the music, lost in her own thoughts and feelings.
When the performance was over, I went up to her and asked her if she liked the music. She opened her eyes and looked at me. Her face was radiant with happiness and peace.

She said in a soft voice, "Thank you. "It has been years since I felt so alive.
From that moment on, I knew I had found what I was meant to do. I started going to nursing homes and retirement communities and telling anyone who would listen how much I loved music.

Over time, I began to notice a big change in the people I played for. People who had been quiet and unresponsive suddenly started tapping their feet and singing along to the familiar songs. Others who had struggled with forgetfulness or dementia seemed to clear their minds as they listened to the music.

I will always remember one man in particular. He used to play jazz, but stiffness prevented him from using his hands. When I first met him, he was sitting alone in his room looking at the wall.

But when I started to play, his face lit up with happiness and recognition. He started humming the tunes, tapping his feet and nodding his head to the music.

He thanked me after the show with tears in his eyes.

"I thought I would never connect with music again," he said. "But you reminded me. Thank you."

As I continue to work with older adults, I am constantly told how music can heal and motivate. Whether it is the familiar melodies of old folk songs or the improvised rhythms of jazz, music can make us feel and remember things that are important to us.
And for older people who may feel alone or forgotten, music can provide a sense of community and connection that is very valuable.

So if you ever feel sad or alone, I recommend that you listen to music. Music can make you feel better and remind you of the beauty and joy of life, whether you play an instrument, sing along to your favorite songs, or just listen to the sounds around you.

32 - The Inheritance of Generosity

Dallas is a city that has undergone many changes over the years. It has faced challenges and setbacks, but it has also experienced tremendous growth and success. One of Dallas' most inspiring stories is that of the Reunion Tower.

The Reunion Tower is an iconic landmark in the city, standing 560 feet tall. It was built in 1978 as part of the revitalization of downtown Dallas. At the time, the city was struggling with economic decline and a negative reputation. The Reunion Tower was seen as a symbol of hope and renewal, a way to bring people back to the city and restore its image.

Over the years, Reunion Tower has become a beloved part of the Dallas skyline. It has undergone several renovations and upgrades, including the addition of an observation deck and restaurant. It has hosted countless events and celebrations and has become a source of pride for the people of Dallas.

The story of Reunion Tower is a testament to the resilience and determination of the people of Dallas. They refused to give up on their city, even in the face of adversity. They saw the potential for growth and success and worked tirelessly to make it a reality.

As a senior, you may have faced your own challenges and setbacks over the years. But the story of Reunion Tower shows that it's never too late to start over, to pursue your dreams, and to make a positive impact on the world around you. So, my friend, I encourage you to be inspired by the people of Dallas and to never give up on your own hopes and aspirations. With determination and perseverance, anything is possible.

33 - Unity in the face of war

The year was 1969 and tensions were high. The Vietnam War was raging and people were protesting in the streets. I had been invited to perform at a peace rally in Central Park, and I was honored to be a part of it.

As I entered the stage, I could feel the energy in the air. The crowd was chanting "Give Peace a Chance," and I knew this was a moment that would go down in history.

I began to play my guitar and sing the words to "Give Peace a Chance. The crowd joined in and soon the entire park was filled with the sound of people singing for peace.

As I looked out over the sea of faces, I saw people from all walks of life. There were young people, old people, black people, white people, and people from all over the world. But at that moment, we were all united in our desire for peace.

After the song ended, I gave a speech about the importance of peace and love. I talked about how we must come together as a global community to end war and violence. I urged the crowd to spread the message of peace and to never give up hope.

As I finished my speech, the crowd erupted in cheers and applause. I could feel the love and energy in the air and I knew we had made a difference.

That day I realized that music has the power to bring people together and inspire change. It didn't matter what our differences were or where we came from. We were all united in our desire for peace.

So if you're ever feeling discouraged about the state of the world, just remember that there are people out there fighting for peace and love. And if we all come together, we can make a difference.

34 - Love Across Generations

There was an elderly woman named Margaret who had always loved spending time with children. She had raised her own children and grandchildren, but as she grew older, she missed the energy and enthusiasm of youth.

One day, Margaret decided to volunteer at the local daycare center. She was nervous at first, but as she walked into the room filled with giggling toddlers, she felt a sense of excitement.

The children, a group of two- and three-year-olds, were playing with blocks and toys. Margaret walked over to a little boy named Tommy and asked if he needed any help.

Tommy looked up at Margaret with his big blue eyes and smiled. "Can you help me build a tower?" he asked.

Margaret sat down next to Tommy and started building. As they worked, Tommy told Margaret about his favorite toys, his friends, and his dreams of becoming a firefighter. Margaret listened intently, feeling a sense of joy she hadn't felt in years.

When the daycare ended, Margaret said goodbye to the children and walked out of the center. As she walked, she realized that even though she was getting older, she still had so much to offer the world. She had a lifetime of experience and wisdom to share, and the children had given her a sense of purpose.

From that day on, Margaret volunteered every week at the daycare center. She played with the children, read them stories, and even taught them how to bake cookies. She became a beloved member of the daycare community, and the children looked forward to seeing her each week.

Margaret realized that even though she was getting older, she still had so much love to give. She found joy in the simple act of spending time with children and discovered that age is just a number.

So if you're ever feeling lonely or disconnected, remember Margaret's story. Take a chance, volunteer at a local daycare or community center, and see where your love and wisdom can take you.

35 - Finding Joy in Old Age

Once upon a time, there was an elderly woman named Margaret who lived in a small town. Margaret had lived a long and full life, but as she grew older, she felt more and more isolated. Her children had moved away, and many of her friends had died.

One day, Margaret decided to take a walk in the city park. As she walked, she noticed a group of children playing on the swings and slides. She smiled as she watched them, remembering the joy of her own childhood.
Suddenly, one of the children ran up to her. "Hi!" said the little girl. "Do you want to play with us?"

Margaret was taken aback. She hadn't played on a swing in years, but something about the child's enthusiasm was contagious. She nodded and followed the little girl to the swings.

As she swung back and forth, Margaret felt a sense of freedom and joy she hadn't felt in years. The children laughed and cheered, and for a moment she felt young again.

After a while, Margaret said goodbye to the children and continued her walk through the park. As she walked, she noticed the beauty of the trees and flowers around her. She realized that even though she was getting older, there was still so much to appreciate in the world.

From that day on, Margaret made it a point to visit the park every week. She played with the children, watched the birds, and enjoyed the simple pleasures of life. She even formed a small gardening club with some of her fellow seniors, and they spent their afternoons tending to the flowers in the park.

Margaret realized that even though she was getting older, she still had so much to offer the world. She found joy in simple things and made new friends along the way. In the process, she discovered that life can be beautiful at any age.

36 - Growing Bolder Not Older

Mrs. Thompson had always dreamed of traveling the world, but she had never had the opportunity. She had spent most of her life taking care of her family and working hard to make ends meet. Now, in her golden years, she felt it was too late to fulfill her dream.

One day, Mrs. Thompson's granddaughter came to visit. She had just returned from a trip to Europe and was eager to share her experiences with her grandmother. As she showed Mrs. Thompson pictures of the Eiffel Tower, the Colosseum and the canals of Venice, Mrs. Thompson felt a sense of longing and regret.

But her granddaughter didn't give up on her dream. She encouraged Mrs. Thompson to start small, to take a trip to a nearby city. She helped her plan the trip, booked a hotel, and even packed her bags.

Mrs. Thompson was nervous at first, but as she boarded the train and watched the scenery pass by, she felt a sense of excitement and adventure. She arrived in the small town and spent the day exploring the local shops and cafes. She met friendly locals who welcomed her with open arms and told her stories about their town.

When Mrs. Thompson returned to her hotel room that night, she felt a sense of accomplishment and pride. She had taken a step outside her comfort zone and discovered a new world of possibilities. She realized that it was never too late to pursue her dreams and that every journey, no matter how small, was a step toward a more fulfilling life.

Over the next few years, Mrs. Thompson continued to travel to new places, each trip more adventurous than the last. She visited national parks, went on cruises, and even traveled to Asia. She felt like a new person, full of energy and curiosity.

As Mrs. Thompson sat in her rocking chair, surrounded by pictures and souvenirs from her travels, she realized that her granddaughter had given her the greatest gift of all: the courage to pursue her dreams and the joy of discovering new places and cultures. She felt grateful for her experiences and knew she would cherish them for the rest of her life.

37 - Upholding Family Ties Despite Bias

Once upon a time, there was an elderly woman named Rose who had recently moved to a retirement home. She missed her old home and her beloved pets, and she felt lonely and isolated in her new surroundings. One day, while sitting in her backyard, she noticed a small flock of birds perched on a nearby tree. The birds were singing a beautiful melody, and Rose was captivated by their sweet voices.

Over the next few days, Rose spent more and more time in the garden, listening to the birds and watching them fly from tree to tree. She began leaving seeds and nuts out for the birds, and soon other birds began coming to the garden. Rose felt a sense of joy and purpose as she watched the birds feed and play in the garden.

One day, as Rose was sitting in the garden, she noticed a small cat walking toward her. The cat was skinny and dirty, and Rose knew she couldn't leave it outside to fend for itself. She took the cat in and gave it a warm bath and a good meal. From that day on, the cat became Rose's constant companion, following her around the nursing home and snuggling with her at night.

As Rose spent more time with her new furry friend, she began to feel more alive and connected to the world around her. She began taking walks in the garden, watching the birds and listening to their songs. She even began volunteering at the retirement home's animal shelter, where she could help care for other animals in need.
Rose realized that even though she was getting older, she

still had so much to give and so much to learn from animals. She was grateful for the joy and companionship they brought to her life, and she knew that as long as she had them by her side, she would never feel alone.

One day, as Rose sat in the garden with her cat, she noticed a group of residents watching her from a distance. They smiled and waved at her, and Rose realized that she had become a source of inspiration and joy to them. She felt proud of the community she had created in the garden, and she knew that the animals had brought them all together.

As Rose sat in the garden, surrounded by the animals she had come to love and the friends she had made, she realized that although she had left her old home behind, she had found a new home in the hearts of those around her.

38 - Intergenerational Connection Through Art

There was an elderly woman who had always had a passion for the arts. She had spent her life attending concerts, visiting museums, and supporting local artists. But as she grew older, she found that her physical limitations made it difficult to continue her involvement in the arts community.

One day, she heard about a program at the Dallas Museum of Art that paired older volunteers with young children interested in learning about art. The woman was hesitant at first, unsure if she had the energy and stamina to work with children. But she decided to give it a try and was paired with a young girl who had never been to a museum before.

The woman and the girl began to meet regularly, exploring the museum's galleries and talking about the artwork. The woman found that she had a natural rapport with the girl, and she enjoyed their time together immensely. She saw how much the girl looked up to her and how much their time together meant to her.

Over time, the woman's health began to improve. She found that her work with the girl gave her a renewed sense of purpose and energy. She began volunteering more often and even started a program to recruit other older volunteers to work with children in need.

The woman realized that her age and physical limitations didn't have to stop her from pursuing her passion for the arts and making a difference in the world. She had found a new way to share her love of art and inspire the next generation of art lovers. And in the process, she had rediscovered her own sense of purpose and joy.

39 - A Philadelphia Story

Philadelphia is a city with a rich history and vibrant culture. It is known for its iconic landmarks, such as the Liberty Bell and Independence Hall, and its thriving arts and music scene. But one of Philadelphia's most inspiring stories is that of the Philadelphia Senior Center.

The Philadelphia Senior Center was founded in 1948 to provide support and resources to the city's elderly population. At the time, many seniors were living in poverty and isolation, with few opportunities for socialization or engagement. The Center was seen as a way to address these issues and improve the quality of life for the city's older adults.

Over the years, the Philadelphia Senior Center has grown and expanded to offer a wide range of programs and services to its members. It offers health and wellness programs, educational classes, social activities, and more. It has become a hub of activity and community for seniors in Philadelphia and has made a tremendous impact on the lives of countless individuals.

One of the most inspiring stories from the Philadelphia Senior Center is that of a woman named Mary. Mary had lived alone for many years, with few friends or family members to rely on. She struggled with depression and loneliness and didn't know where to turn for help.

One day, Mary decided to visit the Philadelphia Senior Center. She was hesitant at first, not sure if she would fit in or enjoy the activities. But she was pleasantly surprised by what she found. The center was filled with friendly and welcoming people, all eager to make new friends and enjoy new experiences.

Mary began attending the center regularly, participating in exercise classes, art workshops, and social events. She found that she had a natural talent for painting and began to create beautiful pieces of art that she proudly displayed around the center. She also made deep connections with the other members, who became like a second family to her.

Over time, Mary's depression lifted and she found a renewed sense of purpose and joy in her life. She became an active and involved member of the Philadelphia Senior Center, volunteering her time and talents to help others. She even started a program to teach other seniors how to paint, sharing her love of art with others.

The story of Mary and the Philadelphia Senior Center is a testament to the power of community and connection. It shows that no matter your age or circumstances, there is always a place for you in the world, and there are always people who care about you and want to help you thrive.

As an older adult in Philadelphia, you may face your own challenges and struggles. But the story of the Philadelphia Senior Center shows that there is hope and support available to you. Whether you're looking for socialization, education, or just a sense of belonging, the Center is here to help.

So my friend, I encourage you to be inspired by Mary's story and reach out to the Philadelphia Senior Center or other community organizations in the city. You never know what kind of connections and opportunities are waiting for you.

40 - Tim & Clara's San Francisco adventures

Clara, an elderly woman, lived in downtown San Francisco. She had lived in the city all her life and watched it change over time. Despite the changes, Clara's affection for San Francisco remained constant.

Tim, Clara's grandson, came to visit her one beautiful day. He noticed that she was depressed and asked her what was bothering her. "I just feel like I'm getting too old for this town," Clara murmured. Things are changing so fast, I can't keep up.

Tim realized his grandmother needed a change of scenery, so he planned a trip around the city to show her a different side of San Francisco. They began by renting bicycles and riding along the Embarcadero, enjoying the ocean breeze and breathtaking views of the water. Clara was amazed by the grandeur of the waterfront and felt a newfound sense of pride in her hometown.

They then rode their bikes to Golden Gate Park, where they spent hours visiting the gardens, museums, and even the bison paddock. Clara had always enjoyed nature, but she had never had the opportunity to visit the park. The beauty and diversity of the flora and fauna amazed her, and she felt a renewed sense of wonder and curiosity.

Tim pointed out all the little details that made San Francisco unique as they pedaled through the city. They stopped for lunch at a food truck, and Clara smiled as she struggled to finish her burrito without spilling the contents all over her lap. They rode their bikes across the Golden Gate Bridge, admiring the iconic structure and feeling the wind in their hair.

Finally, they arrived in the Castro District, where they loved the vibrant atmosphere and vivid murals. Clara felt like she was in another world because of the vibrant neighborhood. "You know, I never realized how much I love this city until today," said Clara as they rode their bikes back to her apartment. Thank you for showing me another side of things.

After that day, Clara began to see San Francisco in a different light. She walked along the ocean, went to museums, and explored other areas. She even started attending events at a nearby community center, something she had always wanted to do but never had the time to do.

Clara made new friends and realized that there was a whole universe of potential waiting for her in San Francisco as she became more involved in the community. She became a member of a senior center, started working at a local library, and felt like she was making a difference in the world.

Clara grew older over the years, but her love for San Francisco remained constant. Even when she couldn't walk as easily as she used to, she'd sit at her window and watch the city go by, grateful for all the memories she'd made there.
When Tim came to visit, they would rent bikes or go to museums, and Clara would tell him stories about the city she adored. No matter what happened, she knew San Francisco would always have a special place in her heart.

41 - Making Memories That Last a Lifetime

Once upon a time, there was an old woman named Edith who had lived in New York City all her life. She had seen the city grow and change over the years, but as she got older, she found it harder and harder to keep up with the fast pace of life in the city.

Edith's niece came to visit her one day and saw that she was sad. Edith sighed and said, "I just feel too old for this city," when the woman asked her what was wrong. Everything is moving so fast that I cannot keep up.

Her granddaughter knew Edith needed a change of pace, so she decided to show her a different side of New York by taking her on a tour of the city. They started with a slow walk through Central Park, where they enjoyed the fresh air and beautiful sights. Edith had always liked the park, but she had never really stopped to enjoy it.

Then they went to the Metropolitan Museum of Art, where

they spent hours looking at paintings and statues. Edith was amazed at how beautiful and creative the art was, and it made her feel curious and amazed all over again.

Edith's granddaughter pointed out all the little things that made New York unique as they walked around the city. They bought hot dogs from a street vendor, which made Edith laugh as she tried to eat hers without getting mustard on her shirt. They were on the subway and heard some jazz artists playing. Edith tapped her foot to the beat.

When they got there, they ate at a small Italian restaurant in Little Italy. Because the food was so good, Edith felt like she was back in her home country. As they walked back to Edith's apartment, she turned to her granddaughter and said, "You know, I didn't realize how much I loved this city until today. You taught me something new about it, so thank you!".

After that day, Edith began to see New York in a different way. She walked in the park, went to museums, and explored different neighborhoods. She even started taking dance classes at a nearby community center, something she had always wanted to do but never had time for.
Edith made new friends and found that New York was full of opportunities as she became more active in the community. She joined a senior center and began volunteering at a nearby hospital. She felt she was making a difference in the world.

As the years went by, Edith got older, but she never stopped loving New York. Even when she couldn't walk as well as she used to, she would sit at her window and watch the city go by, grateful for all the memories she had made there.

When her granddaughter came to visit, they would walk

through the park or go to a museum, and Edith would tell her stories about the city she loved. She knew that no matter what happened, New York would always be very important to her.

42 - Walter's Bocce Ball Benefits

Walter, an elderly man living in a bustling small town, was feeling increasingly lonely as most of his friends had moved away or passed away, and his children were busy with their own lives. He longed for a new activity to fill his days and bring joy back into his life.

One sunny afternoon, Walter decided to visit the town's community center, a place he had always admired from afar but never ventured into. He noticed a group of people gathered in a circle, laughing and clapping. Intrigued, Walter approached the group and discovered that they were members of the local bocce ball club.

The club president, Susan, invited Walter to join the group. Walter was hesitant at first because he had never played bocce before and was unsure of his abilities. However, Susan's infectious enthusiasm and the welcoming smiles of the other members convinced him to give it a try.

As Walter stepped onto the bocce court and began participating in the games, he found himself immersed in the friendly competition and camaraderie of the group. The other members, who ranged in age, shared their own bocce tips and stories, and Walter felt a sense of belonging that he hadn't experienced in a long time.

Over the next few weeks, Walter continued to attend the bocce ball club meetings and found that his loneliness began to fade. He formed close friendships with the other members and discovered a newfound passion for the sport. The laughter and joy he experienced at the club meetings not only lifted his spirits, but also gave him a sense of accomplishment and pride.

One day, as Walter was leaving the community center, he noticed a young man named Jack sitting on a bench, looking down. Remembering how he had felt when he first joined the bocce ball club, Walter approached Jack and invited him to join the group.

With Walter's encouragement and support, Jack soon became an enthusiastic member of the bocce ball club. The two formed a special bond, with Walter sharing his wisdom and life experiences, and Jack bringing a fresh perspective and youthful energy to the group. Together, they worked on their bocce skills and quickly became a formidable team on the court.

As the months passed, the bocce ball club continued to grow, with new members of all ages joining and finding joy in the shared experience of friendly competition. Walter's once empty days were now filled with laughter, friendship, and a sense of purpose.

Walter's story is a reminder that no matter how old we get, we can always find new ways to bring happiness and meaning to our lives. By embracing new experiences, connecting with others, and sharing our wisdom, we can create a lasting legacy that enriches not only our own lives, but the lives of those around us. And sometimes all it takes is a little friendly competition to brighten our days and the days of those around us.

43 - Giggles in the Garden

And sometimes all it takes is a little dirt, a gentle breeze, and a willingness to try something new.

One sunny afternoon, while Evelyn and Lily were working on their butterfly garden, they decided to add a whimsical touch to the space. They painted colorful signs with fun gardening quotes and placed them throughout the garden. The signs brought smiles and laughter to everyone who visited, and soon the garden became known not only for its beauty, but also for its lighthearted atmosphere.

As word of the delightful garden spread, more and more people from the town began to visit, eager to experience the joy and laughter it brought. Garden club members found themselves hosting impromptu garden parties, complete with homemade lemonade and freshly picked vegetables. The garden had become a place where people of all ages could gather, share stories, and enjoy the simple pleasures of life.

One day, a local reporter visited the garden and was so enchanted by its charm and the story of Evelyn and Lily that she wrote an article about it in the town's newspaper. The article caught the attention of a television producer who decided to create a light-hearted gardening show featuring Evelyn, Lily, and the other members of the gardening club.

The show, called "Giggles in the Garden," became an instant hit, with viewers across the country tuning in to watch the heartwarming and humorous adventures of Evelyn, Lily, and their friends. The show's success brought even more visitors to the community garden, and the town soon became known as a destination for those seeking laughter, friendship, and a connection to nature.

Through it all, Evelyn remained humble and grateful for the unexpected turn her life had taken. She continued to mentor Lily and the other members of the garden club, sharing her wisdom and love of gardening with everyone she met. And as she watched the sun set over the garden each evening, she couldn't help but smile, knowing that she had found happiness and purpose in the most unexpected of places.

Evelyn's story is a testament to the power of laughter, friendship, and the simple joys of life. It reminds us that no matter how old we are, we can always find new ways to bring happiness and meaning to our lives. By embracing new experiences, connecting with others, and sharing our wisdom, we can create a lasting legacy that enriches not only our own lives, but the lives of those around us.

So the next time you feel lonely or need a laugh, think of Evelyn and her garden of giggles. Take a chance, try something new, and who knows - you might just find the happiness and purpose you've been searching for hidden among the flowers and laughter of a community garden.

44 - Sand, Sea Breeze, and New Friendships

One day, while Thomas was working on a particularly intricate sandcastle, he noticed a young boy named Max watching him with wide-eyed fascination. Max was new to town and seemed shy and unsure of himself. Remembering how he had felt when he first joined the sand sculpting workshop, Thomas approached Max and invited him to join the group.

With Thomas' guidance and support, Max soon became an enthusiastic member of the sand sculpting workshop. The two formed a special bond, with Thomas sharing his wisdom and life experiences, and Max bringing a fresh perspective and youthful energy to the group. Together they worked on a large sand sculpture depicting a magical underwater kingdom, complete with mermaids, dolphins, and a towering sand castle.

As the months passed, the sand sculpting workshop continued to grow, with new members of all ages joining and finding joy in the shared experience of creating art on the beach. Thomas' once empty days were now filled with laughter, friendship, and a sense of purpose. The beach had become a hub of creativity and unity for the entire town.

In the end, Thomas learned that it's never too late to make new friends, pursue new passions, and find happiness in unexpected places. The sand sculpting workshop not only filled his days with joy, but also gave him a sense of purpose and community that he had been missing for years.

Through his journey, Thomas also discovered the power of mentorship and the importance of passing on his knowledge and experience to the younger generation. His friendship with Max blossomed, and together they continued to make a positive impact on the sand sculpting workshop and the lives of those who participated.

Thomas' story serves as a reminder that no matter our age, we can always find new ways to bring happiness and meaning to our lives. By embracing new experiences, connecting with others, and sharing our wisdom, we can create a lasting legacy that enriches not only our own lives, but also the lives of those around us. And sometimes all it takes is a little sand, a gentle ocean breeze, and a willingness to try something new.

45 - The Garden of Friendship: Evelyn's Story

In a beautiful mountain town lived an elderly woman named Evelyn. She had lived in the town all her life, but as she grew older, she felt increasingly lonely. Most of her friends had either moved away or passed away, and her children were busy with their own lives. Evelyn longed for a new activity to fill her days and bring joy back into her life.

One fall morning, Evelyn decided to visit the town's community garden, a place she had always admired from afar but never ventured into. As she walked through the garden, she marveled at the vibrant colors of the flowers and the delicious scents that filled the air. She noticed a group of people working together, tending to the plants and sharing laughter and conversation.

The group was a local gardening club, led by a kind and knowledgeable man named Henry. Henry noticed Evelyn's interest and invited her to join the group. Evelyn was hesitant at first, but with Henry's gentle encouragement and the welcoming smiles of the other members, she gave it a try.

As Evelyn picked up a trowel and began to plant her first flowers, she found herself immersed in the soothing rhythm of the garden and the camaraderie of the group. The other members, who ranged in age, shared their own gardening tips and stories, and Evelyn felt a sense of belonging that she hadn't experienced in a long time.

Over the next few weeks, Evelyn continued to attend garden club meetings and found that her loneliness began to fade. She formed close friendships with the other members and discovered a newfound passion for gardening. The flowers and vegetables she helped to grow not only beautified the community garden, but also brought a sense of accomplishment and pride to her life.

One day, while tending to her plants, Evelyn noticed a young girl named Lily watching her from the edge of the garden. Lily was new to town and seemed shy and unsure of herself. Remembering how she had felt when she first joined the gardening club, Evelyn approached Lily and invited her to join the group.
With Evelyn's guidance and support, Lily soon became an enthusiastic member of the gardening club. The two formed a special bond, with Evelyn sharing her wisdom and life experiences, and Lily bringing a fresh perspective and youthful energy to the group. Together, they worked on a special project to create a butterfly garden in the community space, attracting beautiful butterflies and providing a serene place for visitors to enjoy.

As the months passed, the garden club continued to grow, with new members of all ages joining and finding joy in the shared experience of caring for the garden. Evelyn's once empty days were now filled with laughter, friendship, and a sense of purpose. The community garden had become a symbol of unity and happiness for the entire town.

Evelyn's story is a reminder that no matter how old we are, we can always find new ways to bring happiness and meaning to our lives. By embracing new experiences, connecting with others, and sharing our wisdom, we can create a lasting legacy that enriches not only our own lives, but also the lives of those around us.

46 - The Beauty of Life: Margaret's Perspective

Margaret sat in her rocking chair and watched the world go by outside her window. The world had changed so much since she was young, and sometimes she wished she could go back to those simpler times.

She remembered the days when she wore rose-colored glasses, a time when everything seemed brighter and simpler. But as she grew older, those glasses seemed to fade away, leaving her to face the world as it really was.
When she looked around her now, she saw a world full of pain and suffering. There were wars and natural disasters, and people seemed to have lost their way. But as she thought about it, she realized that there was still beauty in the world, if you knew where to look.

Margaret thought back to when she was a young woman. She had been so full of hope and dreams, and everything had seemed possible. She had married her high school sweetheart and they had built a life together. They had raised their children and watched them grow up, and now she was surrounded by grandchildren and great-grandchildren.
She had lived a good life, but it hadn't always been easy. She had faced struggles and hardships, but she had always found a way to get through them. And now, as she looked back on her life, she realized that the beauty she had seen through her rose-colored glasses had been there all along.

She had seen it in her husband's smile, in her children's laughter, and in the love of her family. She had seen it in the sunrises and sunsets, in the flowers and trees, and in the stars at night.

As she sat in her rocking chair, Margaret realized that beauty was all around her, if she would only take the time to look for it. She might no longer be wearing rose-colored glasses, but she didn't need them. She had lived a full life, and she had seen the world as it really was.

Drawing on Plato's allegory of the cave, she realized that sometimes people only see what they want to see, or what they are allowed to see. But if they could step out of their comfort zone and look at the world with fresh eyes, they might see things they never knew existed.

Margaret smiled to herself as she rocked back and forth in her chair. She was grateful for the life she had lived, and she was grateful for the beauty she had seen. And she knew that even as she grew older, she would always be able to see the world through rose-colored glasses, as long as she kept her heart open to the beauty that was all around her.

47 - Traditional Tales

Luna has always felt a unique connection to the sea. Her great-grandfather's story of survival in icy waters through a chance encounter with a sea spirit had been passed down through her family for generations. Luna believed she was the chosen one to carry on this mystical guardianship.

One evening, while walking along the shore, Luna spotted a small boat floating in the distance. She ran to take a closer look and saw a young sailor huddled inside, struggling to stay afloat. Without a second thought, she jumped into the water and swam toward the boat, her great-grandfather's story playing in her mind.

As she approached, she could hear the sailor's faint cries for help. Luna pulled him onto her back and swam back to shore as fast as she could. Her family quickly took the sailor to safety, and Luna went home to think about the experience.

The next day, the sailor came to thank Luna and her family for saving his life. Luna explained that she believed she had been sent by a sea spirit to save him. The sailor was skeptical, but grateful.

In time, Luna's story of the sea spirit and her rescue of the sailor became a local legend. People came from far and wide to hear her story and marvel at the young girl's bravery. As Luna grew older, she struggled to balance her personal life with her duties as guardian of the sea. But she remained steadfast in her belief that she was meant to protect those who ventured into the water.

As she approached her twilight years, Luna reflected on the strange turn her life had taken. She had never expected to become a guardian of ancient traditions or a hero to the people of her community. But she was content to know that her great-grandfather's story had come full circle, and that she had fulfilled her duty as the Chosen One.

Luna died peacefully in her sleep, surrounded by her loved ones. Her story continued to be told for generations, each retelling adding a new layer of mysticism and wonder to the tale of the Sea Spirit's guardian.

48 - Secret Letters

Jim and Sarah had a love that transcended time, distance, and tragedy. They were college sweethearts in the 1960s, living at the height of the Vietnam War era. They knew Jim might be drafted, but they vowed to reunite as soon as deployed soldiers returned home.

Their plans were derailed when Jim was drafted and Sarah, who had planned to go with him to California, had to stay behind to care for her ailing mother. Their separation was supposed to be temporary, but unforeseen tragedies kept them apart longer than they anticipated.

Despite the distance and time, they kept their love alive by writing secret letters to each other and hiding them in the books they exchanged. They poured their hearts out in these letters, detailing their hopes and fears, their triumphs and tragedies.

As the years passed, their lives took different paths. Jim returned from the war with PTSD and struggled to adjust to civilian life. He turned to alcohol to numb the pain, and his relationships with others suffered.

Sarah, on the other hand, became a successful businesswoman and married a man who understood and respected her love for Jim. She never forgot her college sweetheart, however, and continued to write to him regularly.

Over the decades, her letters became a reflection of her personal growth and transformation. They mirrored John Keats' theory of negative capacity, as Jim and Sarah were able to embrace uncertainty and ambiguity in their relationship, allowing it to evolve and adapt over time.

One day, Sarah received a phone call from a hospital in California. Jim had been admitted and had no one else to turn to. Sarah immediately flew out to be by his side, and as she sat at his bedside reading the letters he had written her over the years, she realized that their love had never died.

Through all the trials and tribulations they had faced, their love had endured. It was an unexpected reunion under extraordinary circumstances, but they were finally able to be together again.

In the end, Jim and Sarah proved that true love is unbreakable, even in the face of war, distance, and time.

Their love mirrored Langston Hughes' powerful works on diversity and unity, demonstrating that love knows no boundaries and can bring people together, no matter their differences.

49 - Once Forbidden

Maria had grown up in a small desert town where speaking English was forbidden. Her parents, who had immigrated to the United States from Mexico, insisted that Maria and her siblings speak only Spanish to preserve their culture. For years, Maria felt isolated and trapped, unable to connect with the world beyond her community.

As an adult, Maria decided to become an English as a Second Language (ESL) teacher. She wanted to help others who, like her, felt excluded because of language barriers. She began teaching classes to older immigrants in her town, many of whom had come to the United States later in life and were struggling to learn English.

Despite the initial challenge of bridging the language gap, Maria quickly bonded with her students. They shared stories about their home countries and their experiences in the United States. They laughed and studied together, and Maria watched her students gain confidence and independence.

Over time, Maria's health began to fail. She struggled to keep up with the demands of teaching, and her students noticed. They rallied around her, bringing her food and offering to help her teach. Maria was touched by their kindness and felt grateful for the community she had built.

One day, Maria collapsed in the middle of class. Her students rushed to her side and called for an ambulance. As Maria lay in the hospital, she thought about how much her students had meant to her. They had taught her as much as she had taught them, showing her the power of resilience and determination.

Maria's students visited her in the hospital, bringing her flowers and sharing stories of their own experiences with illness and hardship. They sang songs and prayed together, united by their common struggles and triumphs.

In the end, Maria recovered from her illness and returned to teaching. But she was changed by the experience. She realized that love and connection can transcend any barrier, be it language, culture, or illness. She was grateful for her students and the lessons they had taught her, and she felt inspired to continue helping others bridge the gaps that had once isolated her.
In the spirit of Langston Hughes' powerful works on diversity and unity, Maria's story shows us that we are all connected, regardless of our differences. Through love, empathy and understanding, we can build bridges and create a more compassionate world.

50 - Inseparable Shadows

Mary had lived a long and full life with her beloved husband, William. They had raised three children, traveled the world, and experienced countless joys and sorrows together. But when William died a few years ago, Mary felt as if a part of her had died as well.

One day, while sorting through old boxes in the attic, Mary came across a faded piece of paper with William's handwriting on it. As she read the words, tears streamed down her face and she felt a surge of emotion she had not felt in a long time. It was a love poem he had written for her when they were young and in love.

Over the next few weeks, Mary often took out the poem and read it over and over again. She felt as if William's spirit was with her, whispering sweet nothings in her ear. Memories of their early years together flooded back, and she relived each moment as if it were happening again.

One evening, Mary decided to attend a poetry reading at a local bookstore. As she listened to the poets recite their verses, she felt inspired to share William's poem with the audience. With a shaky voice, she stood up and read the words aloud, tears streaming down her face.

The crowd was moved by the power and beauty of the poem, and many approached Mary afterward to express their condolences and admiration for her and William's enduring love. Some even shared their own love stories, and Mary felt she had connected with a community of kindred spirits.

Encouraged by this experience, Mary decided to compile a book of love poems, including William's, to share with others. She spent countless hours poring over old books, searching for the perfect words to capture the essence of love and devotion.

As she worked on the project, Mary realized that love is not something that dies with the person, but rather something that lives on in the memories and hearts of those it touches. She felt grateful for the time she had spent with William and for the opportunity to share their love story with others.

Years later, as Mary sat in her rocking chair, surrounded by her children, grandchildren, and great-grandchildren, she knew that William's love had never left her. It had been with her all along, a shining light in the darkness and a reminder that love is indeed eternal.

51 - Dancing Memories

Ed and Marion had been married for over 60 years and their love was as strong as ever. They had always enjoyed dancing together, especially ballroom dancing. Every week they attended a dance class at their local community center, reliving memories of their courtship.

But as they grew older, Marion began to experience cognitive decline. She struggled to remember even the simplest steps, and her memories of their past together began to fade. It was a painful realization for both of them, but Ed remained steadfast and determined to continue dancing with his beloved wife.

He would gently guide her through the steps, holding her close and whispering in her ear. He would remind her of their first dance, their wedding, and the birth of their children. Even though Marion could no longer remember those moments, Ed made sure they were still present in her heart.

Despite the difficulties, they continued to attend weekly dance classes. They became a beloved fixture among the other seniors, admired for their dedication and the beauty of their dancing. They even performed one last dance for their family and friends, a touching moment of love and togetherness that brought tears to everyone's eyes.

As they embraced and swayed to the rhythm of the music, Ed whispered to Marion, "Remember the first time we danced to this song?" Marion smiled and replied, "I do now, my love. I do now."

Their love and the power of dance had overcome the challenges of aging and cognitive decline. And though their memories may have faded, their connection and passion for each other remained strong to the end.

52 - Finding Joy in The Simple Things

Once upon a time, there was an elderly woman named Ruth who lived alone in a small house in the country. She had lived a long and full life, but lately she had felt lonely and isolated. Her children and grandchildren visited her occasionally, but she longed for more companionship.

One day, Ruth decided to plant a garden in her backyard. She had always loved gardening and thought it would be a great way to keep busy and enjoy the fresh air. She worked hard every day, planting flowers, vegetables, and herbs.

While tending to her garden, she noticed that she wasn't alone. A small bird had made a nest in one of her trees and visited her every day. Ruth enjoyed the bird's company and looked forward to her visits.

One day Ruth discovered that the bird had laid eggs in its nest. She was overjoyed and watched the bird carefully, making sure it had everything it needed to raise its babies. She even called the bird "Mama" and felt a special bond with her.

As the days passed, Ruth watched the eggs hatch and the baby birds grow stronger. She marveled at the bond between Mama and her babies and was filled with a sense of wonder and awe.

One morning, as Ruth tended to her garden, she heard a noise behind her. She turned to see Mama and her babies perched on a nearby branch, chirping happily. Ruth smiled and felt a deep sense of contentment wash over her. She realized that even though she lived alone, she was never really alone. She had Mama and her babies, and she had her beautiful garden.

From that day forward, Ruth spent every morning tending her garden and spending time with Mama and her babies. She was grateful for their companionship and for the beauty of nature that surrounded her. She knew that no matter how lonely she might sometimes feel, she could always find comfort and joy in the simple pleasures of life.

And so, dear reader, I hope Ruth's story has brought a smile to your face and reminded you that even in the darkest of times, there is always something to be thankful for. Whether it's a garden, a pet, or a simple act of kindness, there is beauty and love all around us, if only we take the time to look for it.

53 - The Power of Positive Thinking

As a young girl, Lily was always told that she could do anything she set her mind to. Her parents instilled in her a sense of confidence and determination that helped her believe in herself and her abilities.

But as she grew older and faced the challenges of adulthood, Lily began to doubt herself. She had dreams and aspirations, but she wasn't sure she had what it took to achieve them.

One day, she found herself at a crossroads. She had been offered a job opportunity that would allow her to pursue her passions and make a difference in the world, but it was a risky move. It meant leaving behind the security and stability of her current job and taking a leap of faith into the unknown.

Lily's parents could see the fear in her eyes and knew she

needed some encouragement. So they shared a story from their own past.

When they were young and just starting out, they too had faced a difficult decision. They had the opportunity to start their own business, but it meant leaving their steady jobs and taking a chance on something new.

They had been scared, just like Lily was now. But they had taken the risk, and it had paid off. Their business had flourished, and they had built a life they were proud of.

As Lily listened to their story, she felt a sense of comfort and reassurance. If her parents could take a risk and make it work, maybe she could, too.

With their support and encouragement, Lily took the leap. She took the job opportunity and put all her energy into it. It was a difficult road, with many setbacks and challenges along the way, but she persevered.

And in the end, it was all worth it. She had found her calling and was making a difference in the world. Lily realized that the only thing standing in her way was her own self-doubt, and that she had the strength and courage to overcome it.

Thanks to her parents' encouragement, Lily had found the confidence to take a chance on herself, and it had paid off in ways she never could have imagined.

54 - Summer Memories

As I sat in my rocking chair, I couldn't help but think about the past. Memories flooded my mind and I couldn't help but smile as I remembered the good times.

I remembered the long summer days spent playing outside with my siblings, the sound of laughter echoing through the yard. We ran through the sprinklers, caught fireflies at night, and lay in the grass watching the clouds pass by. Life was so simple then, and I didn't have a care in the world.

I also thought about my parents who worked so hard to give us a good life. They didn't have much, but they always made sure we had enough to eat and clothes on our backs. They worked long hours and sacrificed so much for us, and I am forever grateful.

As I got older, life got more complicated. There were bills to pay, jobs to worry about, and responsibilities that never seemed to end. But even in the midst of it all, I found joy in the little things. A good book, a hot cup of tea, a walk in the park. Those little moments of peace kept me going, even when things felt overwhelming.

Now, as I sit here in my old age, I realize how quickly time has passed. It seems like only yesterday that I was a carefree child playing in the sun, but now I am a wrinkled old woman with a lifetime of memories behind me.

But even though I am old, I am not sad. I am grateful for the life I have lived, and I am content knowing that I have loved and been loved in return. The memories of my past are like a warm blanket that I can wrap around me when I feel lonely or sad. They remind me of all the good in the world, even when things seem dark.

So I sit here in my rocking chair, watching the world go by outside my window, and I am at peace. Life may not always be easy, but it is always beautiful, and I am grateful for every moment of it.

55 - The Power of Positivity

Once upon a time, there was a young woman named Sarah who had always dreamed of becoming a nurse. She loved the idea of helping people, but life had thrown her a few curveballs that made it seem like that dream might never come true.

First, her parents became ill and she had to drop out of college to care for them. Then, when they passed away, she struggled to find steady work and ended up taking a job at a fast-food restaurant just to make ends meet.

But Sarah never gave up on her dream. She continued to take classes online and read every book she could about nursing. She even spent her free time volunteering at a local hospital, just to be around the environment she hoped to one day work in.

One day, while serving customers at the restaurant, a woman came in who looked like she was in distress. Sarah could tell something was wrong, so she went over to talk to her.

The woman explained that her son had just been admitted to the hospital and she didn't know what to do. She was new to the area and had no family nearby to help her. Sarah listened patiently and then offered to go with her to the hospital to see if she could help in any way.

When they arrived, Sarah quickly realized that the woman's son was in the same ward where she was volunteering. She introduced the woman to the charge nurse and explained the situation. The nurse was grateful for the help, and Sarah stayed with the woman until her son was settled and comfortable.

As they left the hospital, the woman turned to Sarah and said, "You are an angel. You helped us when we needed it most. Sarah was moved by the woman's words and realized that helping others was what she was meant to do.

Not long after that encounter, Sarah received an acceptance letter to nursing school. She worked hard, graduated with honors, and soon landed a job at the same hospital where she had volunteered for so long.

Sarah never forgot the woman who called her an angel. She knew she had been sent to that fast-food restaurant that day for a reason-to help someone in need and to remember why she had always wanted to be a nurse.

From that day forward, Sarah made it her mission to help others whenever she could, and she felt fulfilled and grateful for the opportunity to live her dream.

56 - The Power of Perseverance: A Sports Story

It was a sunny day, and the local high school basketball team was getting ready to play their biggest rival. The team had been practicing hard for months, and the players were determined to win the game.

The atmosphere was electric as the game began. The crowd was cheering for their team, and the players were putting everything they had into every play. It was a close game, with both teams fighting hard for the win.

As the final minutes of the game approached, the score was tied. The tension in the air was palpable, and the players on both teams were exhausted. But in the midst of all the chaos, one player stood out.

Johnny, a senior on the high school team, had been a

consistent performer all season. He was known for his determination and never-say-die attitude. With just seconds left on the clock, Johnny made a move that surprised everyone.

He took a risky shot from beyond the three-point line and it went in! The crowd erupted in cheers as Johnny's teammates mobbed him on the court. The final buzzer sounded and the high school team had won the game.

The players and coach were ecstatic. They had worked so hard for this moment, and it had finally paid off. But the most rewarding moment for Johnny came when he looked up into the stands and saw his parents beaming with pride.

Johnny had grown up in a tough neighborhood and had faced many challenges in his life. But he had found solace in basketball and had worked tirelessly to improve his skills. This win was not only a victory for the team, but also a symbol of Johnny's perseverance and determination.

As the team celebrated their victory, Johnny felt grateful for all the hard work he had put in. He knew that the lessons he learned on the court would stay with him for the rest of his life.

57 - A Helping Hand

Once upon a time, there was a little girl named Lily who loved to dance. She spent hours twirling and jumping around her room, imagining herself on stage as a beautiful ballerina.

But Lily had a problem - she was born with a physical disability that made it difficult for her to move like other children her age. Her parents worried that her love of dance would be stifled by her limitations.

But Lily was determined to find a way to dance despite her disability. She began attending dance classes specially designed for children with physical disabilities, and she worked hard every day to improve her movements and build her strength.

As she grew older, Lily's love of dance grew stronger. She auditioned for a local dance company and was overjoyed when she was accepted. She spent countless hours rehearsing and perfecting her routines, never giving up her dream of becoming a professional dancer.

Finally, the day of the big performance arrived. Lily was nervous but excited as she walked out on stage in her costume. The music began and she danced her heart out, her movements graceful and fluid.

As the audience cheered and applauded, tears filled Lily's eyes. She had done it - she had overcome her disability and achieved her dream of becoming a dancer.

From that day on, Lily continued to dance and inspire others with disabilities to pursue their passions. She proved that with hard work and determination, anything is possible.

58 - Memories on Wheels

In a small town nestled among rolling hills, there was an old garage with a reputation for restoring classic cars to their former glory. The shop had been there for decades, and the owner, a grizzled old mechanic named Hank, had been fixing cars since he was a young man.

Hank loved nothing more than the sound of an engine

purring under his fingertips. He had a special fondness for old cars that had seen better days, and he would often spend months, sometimes years, restoring them to their former glory.

One day, a young man named Jack walked into Hank's garage. Jack had inherited his grandfather's old Mustang, but it was in terrible shape. The paint was chipped and faded, and the engine wouldn't start.
Hank took one look at the Mustang and knew he had his work cut out for him. But he saw the same passion for old cars in Jack's eyes that he had seen in himself when he was younger, and he decided to take on the project.

For months, Hank worked tirelessly on the Mustang, pouring his heart and soul into every detail. He replaced the engine, sanded down the rust, and gave the car a fresh coat of paint. When he was done, the Mustang looked like it had just rolled off the assembly line.

Jack was overjoyed to see the finished product. He couldn't believe that the car he once thought was beyond repair could look so beautiful.
As Jack drove away in his newly restored Mustang, Hank couldn't help but feel a sense of pride and satisfaction. He knew that he had helped keep a piece of history alive, and that the car he had restored would continue to bring joy to its owner for years to come.

From that day on, Jack became a regular customer at Hank's shop, bringing in his friends' old cars for restoration. And Hank continued to work his magic, restoring old cars and bringing them back to life, one engine at a time.

59 - The Ripple Effect of Good Deeds

Once upon a time, there was a man named John who had always dreamed of opening his own bakery. He had a passion for baking since childhood and spent countless hours experimenting in the kitchen.

After years of saving money and perfecting his recipes, John finally decided to take the plunge and open his own bakery. He spent months preparing and planning, and finally opened his doors to the public.

Things were slow at first. John struggled to attract customers and worried that his dream of owning a successful bakery might not come true. But he didn't give up. He continued to perfect his recipes and worked tirelessly to make his bakery the best it could be.

Slowly but surely, word of John's delicious pastries and breads began to spread. People began to come from all over town to sample his creations. John was overjoyed and overwhelmed by the positive response.

As the months went by, John's bakery became more and more popular. He hired a team of talented bakers and expanded his menu to include new and exciting treats. His business grew and flourished, and he was finally able to live his dream of being a successful bakery owner.

But for John, the most gratifying part of owning his bakery wasn't the financial success. It was the joy he brought to his customers. He loved to see their faces light up with happiness as they bit into his sweet and savory creations.

John had never felt more fulfilled. He had taken a risk and followed his passion, and it had paid off in ways he could never have imagined. Every day, he woke up excited to go to work and share his love of baking with the world.

Looking back on his journey, John knew that the long hours and hard work had been worth it. He was grateful for the opportunity to live his dream and make a positive difference in the lives of others. And he knew that he would continue to bake with passion and love for the rest of his life.

60 - San Francisco: The City That Keeps on Giving

San Francisco is a city known for its beauty, diversity and vibrant culture. It's a place where people from all walks of life come together to create something special. And for an elderly woman named Rose, San Francisco was the place she had called home for more than 50 years.

Rose had seen the city change a lot over the years, but she still loved it as much as when she first arrived. She loved the hills, the ocean, and the colorful neighborhoods that made San Francisco so unique.

One day, Rose's granddaughter came to visit her and noticed that she seemed a little down. When asked what was wrong, Rose sighed and said, "I just feel like I'm getting too old for this city. Everything is changing so fast, and I can't keep up.

Her granddaughter knew Rose needed a change of pace, so she decided to take her on a tour of the city that would show her a different side of San Francisco. They started with a ride on the famous cable cars, taking in the breathtaking views of the city from the top of the hills. Rose was amazed by the beauty and grandeur of the city and felt a renewed sense of pride in her hometown.

Next they went to Golden Gate Park, where they spent

hours exploring the gardens and museums. Rose had always loved nature, but she had never had the opportunity to visit the park. She was amazed by the beauty and variety of plants and animals, and she felt a renewed sense of wonder and curiosity.

As they walked around the city, Rose's granddaughter pointed out all the little things that make San Francisco special. They stopped at a bakery for coffee and pastries, and Rose laughed as she tried to eat her croissant without getting crumbs on her shirt. They took the ferry to Alcatraz Island and learned about the history of the famous prison, and Rose felt like she was traveling back in time.

Finally, they landed in Chinatown, where they had dinner at a bustling Chinese restaurant. The food was delicious, and Rose felt like she was in another world. As they walked back to Rose's apartment, she turned to her granddaughter and said, "You know, I never realized how much I love this city until today. Thank you for showing me another side of it.

From that day on, Rose began to see San Francisco in a new light. She took walks along the ocean, visited museums, and explored different neighborhoods. She even started taking dance classes at a local community center, something she had always wanted to do but never had the time.

As she became more involved in the community, Rose made new friends and discovered that there was a world of opportunity waiting for her in San Francisco. She joined a senior center, started volunteering at a local hospital, and felt like she was making a difference in the world.

As the years passed and Rose grew older, she never lost her love for San Francisco. Even when she couldn't walk as easily as she used to, she would sit at her window and watch the city go by, grateful for all the memories she had made there.

And whenever her granddaughter came to visit, they would take a ride on the cable cars or visit a museum, and Rose would tell her stories about the city she loved. She knew that no matter what happened, San Francisco would always have a special place in her heart.

61 - Heaven Sent Messenger

Once upon a time, there was an elderly man named Harold who had lived in Chicago all his life. He had seen the city go through many changes over the years, but he still loved it just as much as when he was a young man.

One day, Harold's granddaughter came to visit him and noticed that he seemed a little down. When she asked him what was wrong, Harold sighed and said, "I just feel like I'm getting too old for this town. Everything is changing so fast, and I can't keep up.

His granddaughter knew Harold needed a change of pace, so she decided to take him on a tour of the city that would show him a different side of Chicago. They started with a ride on the famous Chicago River Architecture Tour, where they learned about the history and design of the city's iconic buildings. Harold was amazed by the beauty and grandeur of the architecture and felt a renewed sense of pride in his hometown.

Next, they went to the Art Institute of Chicago, where they spent hours admiring the paintings and sculptures. Harold had always loved art, but he had never had the opportunity to visit the museum. He was amazed by the talent and creativity of the artists and felt a renewed sense of wonder and curiosity.

As they walked around the city, Harold's granddaughter pointed out all the little things that made Chicago special. They stopped at a hot dog stand and had lunch, and Harold laughed as he tried to eat his hot dog without getting ketchup all over his shirt. They rode the L train and listened to a group of musicians playing the blues, and Harold tapped his foot to the beat.

Eventually they ended up in Chinatown, where they had dinner at a busy Chinese restaurant. The food was delicious, and Harold felt like he was in another world. As they walked back to Harold's apartment, he turned to his granddaughter and said, "You know, I never realized how much I love this city until today. Thank you for showing me another side of it.

From that day on, Harold began to see Chicago in a new light. He took walks along the lakefront, visited museums, and explored different neighborhoods. He even started taking cooking classes at a local community center, something he had always wanted to do but never had the time.

As he became more involved in the community, Harold made new friends and discovered that there was a whole world of opportunities waiting for him in Chicago. He joined a senior center, started volunteering at a local food bank, and felt like he was making a difference in the world.

Years passed and Harold grew older, but he never lost his love for Chicago. Even when he couldn't walk as easily as he used to, he would sit at his window and watch the city go by, grateful for all the memories he had made there.

And whenever his granddaughter came to visit, they would take a ride on the river or visit a museum, and Harold would tell her stories about the city he loved. He knew that no matter what happened, Chicago would always have a special place in his heart.

62 - Frozen Love Flowers

Mrs. Lee was used to the cold of the harsh Boston winter, but the frost of her neighbor's heart still caught her off guard. Mr. Nakamura was an elderly Japanese war veteran who lived alone in the apartment across the hall. Despite her attempts at friendly conversation, he always gave her a cold stare and said nothing.
One day, Mrs. Lee noticed that Mr. Nakamura had not picked up his mail for several days. Concerned, she knocked on his door, but there was no answer. She tried again the next day, but there was still no answer. Finally, on the third day, she called the building manager, who agreed to open Mr. Nakamura's apartment with a spare key.
Mrs. Lee was shocked by the condition of Mr. Nakamura's apartment. It was filthy, and he was lying on the floor in obvious discomfort. She immediately called an ambulance and stayed with him at the hospital until his condition stabilized.
From that day on, Mr. Nakamura's attitude toward Mrs. Lee changed. He became more friendly and they even began to talk. Mrs. Lee learned that Mr. Nakamura had been a Japanese soldier during World War II and had been captured by American forces. He had spent several years in a prisoner of war camp, and the memories haunted him to this day.
Mrs. Lee, herself an immigrant from China, understood the

trauma of war all too well. Her father had fought for the Chinese army during the Second Sino-Japanese War and had suffered greatly. She shared some of her own experiences with Mr. Nakamura, and he gradually began to open up to her.

As they talked more, Mrs. Lee learned that Mr. Nakamura had a passion for traditional Japanese calligraphy and origami. She remembered how her own father had taught her the art of Chinese calligraphy when she was a child. She offered to teach Mr. Nakamura some Chinese calligraphy techniques, and he accepted.

They spent many afternoons together practicing their art, sharing their stories, and even folding origami flowers. Mrs. Lee would often bring fresh flowers from the local market, and they would fold paper flowers together, imagining their favorite flowers blooming again in the spring.

Eventually, Mr. Nakamura's health took a turn for the worse. Mrs. Lee visited him in the hospital every day, bringing him small gifts and talking to him. One day, Mr. Nakamura told her a secret: During the war, he had fallen in love with a Chinese woman who worked for the resistance. They had met in secret and exchanged letters until the end of the war, when he had to return to Japan.

Mrs. Lee was moved by Mr. Nakamura's story and promised to help him find his lost love. Together they searched for any clues they could find and eventually discovered that the woman was still alive and living in China. They wrote to her, and to their surprise, she replied. They arranged a video call, and Mr. Nakamura and his lost love were able to speak for the first time in over seventy years.

After Mr. Nakamura's death, Mrs. Lee took comfort in knowing that she had helped him find closure and reconnect with his lost love. She continued to fold origami flowers and practice calligraphy, but always felt a sense of loss in her heart. However, every time she saw a paper flower or a piece of calligraphy, she was reminded of the bond she shared with Mr. Nakamura and the beauty they had created together, frozen in time like love flowers preserved in ice.

63 - Twice Upon a Memory

As the family walked the cobblestone streets of Paris, the grandmother couldn't help but feel a rush of nostalgia as she recognized familiar sights from her youth. She told her grandchildren about the time she was a young woman, a nurse during World War II, and fell in love with a brave French resistance fighter named Luc.

"He was my first love," she said, "we were both so young and caught up in the excitement of the war. We promised each other we would be together when it was over."

The grandchildren listened intently as their grandmother recounted her adventures with Luc, the days when they met secretly in hidden places around the city. She described how their love blossomed despite the danger that surrounded them.

As they wandered the streets, they came upon the grandmother's old neighborhood. Her eyes lit up with recognition as she pointed out her former apartment building. The family entered a nearby cafe, and Grandmother's gaze drifted to an elderly man sitting alone at a nearby table. His eyes met hers, and suddenly she gasped.

"Luc!" she exclaimed.

The man stood up, and the grandmother rushed over to hug him. The grandchildren watched in amazement as the two old lovers held each other tightly, tears streaming down their faces. They sat down and talked for hours, reminiscing about their past and catching up on their lives since they had last seen each other. The grandmother introduced her grandchildren to Luc, and they all shared a meal together, laughing and talking like old friends.

When the family returned to their hotel that night, the grandmother's heart was filled with joy. She had never expected to see Luc again, let alone in her old neighborhood in Paris. She told her grandchildren that their meeting had brought back memories she thought were lost forever.

"Memory is a funny thing," she said. "It can be both a burden and a blessing. But it's moments like this that remind me how beautiful it can be to remember a time and a love that was so pure and true."

The grandchildren listened, and as they drifted off to sleep that night, they thought about the love story that had unfolded before them. They knew it was a story they would remember for the rest of their lives, a story of love that had transcended time and distance, a story of two people who had found each other twice in memory.

64 - Never Too Late for Love

Every Tuesday, Max, a young musician, visited the nursing home to lead a sing-along with the residents. Max was always fascinated by the stories they shared, but he had a special fondness for Miss Elsie, a gentle soul in her eighties. One day, Max decided to form an intergenerational choir and invited young volunteers from his music school to join the weekly singing sessions. The residents were thrilled to meet the enthusiastic young singers, and Max was happy to see everyone enjoying themselves.

As the weeks went by, Max and Miss Elsie grew closer. They often chatted after the sing-alongs, sharing their favorite songs and memories. Max loved hearing about Miss Elsie's life and the experiences that shaped her.

One day, while discussing their family history, Max and Miss Elsie discovered a surprising connection. Max's great-grandfather had been a soldier in World War II and had fought alongside Miss Elsie's husband.
Over the next few weeks, Max and Miss Elsie's friendship blossomed into something more. They began taking walks in the park, enjoying each other's company and sharing their passions. Max loved playing his guitar for Miss Elsie, and she loved singing along to his favorite songs.

One day, Max surprised Miss Elsie by bringing his guitar to the nursing home and playing a special song for her. As he played Louis Armstrong's "What a Wonderful World," Miss Elsie's eyes lit up and tears streamed down her face.

Max knew then that he had found someone very special in Miss Elsie. Age had no bearing on the love and happiness they shared, and he was grateful for the chance to have met her. As Louis Armstrong once sang, it truly was a wonderful world, and it was never too late for love.

65 - Unbreakable Bonds

Living alone, a centenarian begins writing messages to those who have touched her life through significant milestones. From childhood friends to past lovers, she addresses each letter to a place and time meant only for

her.
or her. As she writes, she reflects on the lasting impact they had on her and how they helped shape the person she is today.

Despite the lack of response, the act of writing brings her immense joy and a sense of connection to those who have long since passed. Each letter is a testament to the unbreakable bonds that were formed and how they continue to influence her life, even after all these years.

One day, a young couple moves into the neighborhood and discovers an old box of letters hidden in their attic. Intrigued, they read through them, and to their surprise, they realize they have a connection to the writer.

They find the centenarian and introduce themselves, and she is overjoyed to have someone to share her stories with in person. They listen intently as she recounts her life, and they quickly become friends.

Through the letters and their conversations, the three realize that despite their very different life experiences, they share a common bond of love and connection to the people they care about. They understand that while time may pass, the memories and love they hold will always be unbreakable bonds.

66 - A Time Before Us

Lena and Jack stood before their family and friends, holding hands and looking into each other's eyes. After 57 years of marriage, they had decided to renew their vows.

As they exchanged words of love and commitment, memories of their long journey together flooded back. They recalled the early days of their marriage when they struggled to make ends meet while raising their three children. They remembered the times when they fought and disagreed, but always found their way back to each other.

They remembered the happy moments they shared, like the day they bought their first house and the joy of watching their children grow up and start families of their own. They also remembered the difficult times, like when Jack lost his job and Lena had to work long hours to support them.

At the end of the ceremony, they gathered with their loved ones to celebrate their enduring love. Lena and Jack asked their friends to share their own reflections on love and relationships.
Their friends spoke about the importance of communication, forgiveness, and understanding. They talked about how their own relationships had grown and evolved over the years and offered words of wisdom to the couple.

As the evening drew to a close, Lena and Jack hugged their friends and family, grateful for the support and love they had received over the years. They walked out hand in hand, their hearts overflowing with joy and gratitude for the time they had shared.

For Lena and Jack, renewing their vows was not only a celebration of their love, but also a reminder of the journey they had taken together. They knew that life was not always easy, but they also knew that their love had endured and would continue to endure through all of life's ups and downs.

67 - From one heart to another

William had always been fascinated by medicine and the advances it brought. Even in his old age, he was enthusiastic about donating his heart to science when he died. He knew he wouldn't be around to see the effects of his donation, but he was content with the thought of helping others through his death.

When William died, his heart was given to a young woman named Elise, who had a congenital heart defect. Elise was overjoyed with the gift and grateful for the chance to live longer. As she recovered from the transplant, however, she began to experience strange, vivid dreams that felt like memories. She dreamed of a man she had never met and experienced moments of his life that felt as real as her own.

The dreams continued, and Elise became curious about the man in her dreams. She searched for information about her heart donor and eventually discovered William's name. She contacted his family and learned more about him. They shared stories and memories, and Elise felt like she was getting to know the man who had given her a second chance at life.

But then something unexpected happened. William's voice began to creep into Elise's dreams. At first it was just a murmur, but soon it grew louder and more distinct. He spoke to her, telling her about his life and experiences, sharing his joys and sorrows.

Elise was startled but fascinated. She felt she was getting to know William on an even deeper level. She realized that their connection went beyond the physical heart transplant. It was as if their souls were intertwined.

As the months passed, Elise and William's connection grew

stronger. She found comfort in his voice and stories, and he found peace in knowing that a part of him was still alive and thriving.

Eventually, Elise realized that she had fallen in love with William, even though she had never met him in person. She wasn't sure how to approach the subject, but she knew she had to tell his family about the connection she felt with their loved one.
When she finally told them, they were moved by the depth of her feelings. They had always known that William was a special man, but they had no idea that his heart would continue to touch lives even after his death.
Elise and William's family became close, sharing memories and stories about the man they all loved. They knew that William would have been overjoyed to know that his gift had brought so much love and connection to the world.

As Elise continued to dream of William, she felt his presence with her always. She knew that his heart was beating in her chest, and she was grateful for the opportunity to keep his memory alive.

In the end, William and Elise's bond showed that love knows no boundaries, not even those of life and death. As Edgar Allan Poe once wrote, "The boundaries that separate life from death are at best shadowy and vague. Who can say where one ends and the other begins?"

68 - Enchanted Moonlight Serenade

It was a crisp autumn evening when the two strangers first met. The park was empty, save for the occasional rustling of leaves and the soft glow of street lamps in the distance. She was an elderly woman, bundled up in a warm coat and hat, sitting on a bench, staring up at the sky. He was a young man, no more than thirty, wandering aimlessly through the park.

As he passed the bench, she looked up and their eyes met. There was a moment of recognition, as if they had known each other before. He stopped and asked if she needed any help, and she replied that she was just enjoying the night sky. They fell into conversation easily, as if they were old friends catching up after years apart.

He asked her if she liked music, and she smiled and replied that she was a fan of Glenn Miller. Without hesitation, he pulled out his phone and played "Moonlight Serenade". The soft strains of the music filled the air, transporting them both to another time and place.

Under the moonlight, they began to share their stories. She told him of her youth during the war, of dancing with her lover to this very song. He told her of his failed relationships, of the heartbreak that had left him feeling lost and alone.
As they talked, they felt a connection grow between them, a bond that transcended age and circumstance. They were just two people sharing a moment of peace and understanding under the enchanted moonlight.

As the song ended, they both knew it was time to say goodbye. He thanked her for the conversation and promised to visit again. She smiled and wished him well, grateful for the unexpected company.

From that night on, they met regularly in the park, always under the moon and always with "Moonlight Serenade" playing softly in the background. They talked about everything and nothing, enjoying each other's company and the simple pleasure of being alive.

In a world that had become increasingly disconnected and fast-paced, they had found each other, two souls united by the magic of music and the wonder of the night sky. And even as the seasons changed and time passed, they continued to share their enchanted moonlight serenade, a reminder that even in the darkest of nights, there is always hope for connection and love.

69 - Wildflowers in Winter

As the winter winds blew, the retired botanist ventured into the nearby woods, hoping to find solace in the quiet beauty of nature. It had been months since her beloved husband had died of Alzheimer's disease, and she was still struggling to come to terms with her loss.
As she walked through the woods, she spotted a patch of wildflowers peeking out from under the snow. She knelt down to take a closer look, and as she did, memories of her husband flooded back.

They had both been botany students at the nearby university, and it was during a winter hike in these very woods that they had fallen in love. They had spent countless hours exploring the woods and fields, discovering new plants and species together.

Now, as she gazed at the wildflowers before her, she felt her husband's presence all around her. She closed her eyes and breathed in the crisp winter air, feeling a sense of peace and calm come over her.

For the rest of the winter, the botanist visited the wildflowers every day. She watched as they slowly began to bloom and thrive despite the harsh winter conditions, and she marveled at their resilience and beauty.

Through the wildflowers, she found a renewed sense of purpose and joy, and she knew that her husband would be proud of her for continuing to explore and appreciate the wonders of nature.

As winter began to fade and the first signs of spring appeared, the botanist knew that she would always carry her husband's memories with her, just as the wildflowers would always carry the promise of new life and growth.

70 - Forbidden Melody

In a small village in Andalusia, Spain, where the sounds of flamenco filled the air, lived a young man named Manuel. He was an amateur guitarist, but his passion for music was evident in every strum. He played for hours every day, sometimes for himself, sometimes for his friends in the plaza.

One day, Manuel heard the sound of gunfire coming from the hills. The Spanish Civil War had reached his village, and he knew he had to help. He joined a local militia and was sent to the front lines.

There he met a beautiful woman named Maria. She fought alongside her husband, but she had a secret passion for music. Manuel and Maria shared a love of music and spent many evenings singing and playing guitar around the campfire.

As their friendship grew, Manuel found himself falling in love with Maria. He knew it was forbidden, but he couldn't help his feelings. Maria was also attracted to Manuel, but she was torn between her love for her husband and her growing affection for the young guitarist.

One day, while they were playing together, they were discovered by Maria's husband. He was furious and threatened to report Manuel to the authorities. Manuel knew he had to leave the camp and go into hiding.

Days turned into weeks, and Manuel longed to see Maria again. He composed a song about their forbidden love, hoping it would reach her ears and let her know how he felt. He played the song everywhere he went, hoping it would find its way to Maria.

Finally, one day, Maria appeared before him. She had left her husband and had come to find him. They embraced and shared a tender kiss. Manuel played the song he had written for her, and they danced together under the stars.

Their love was short-lived, however, as the war raged on. One day, Maria was killed in battle, and Manuel was heartbroken. He left Spain and traveled the world, playing his guitar and singing the song he had written for Maria.

Years passed, and Manuel returned to his village, now an old man. He went to the plaza where he had played for so many years and began to play his guitar again. As he played the song he had written for Maria, he felt her spirit beside him, dancing to the forbidden melody.

71 - Two Paths Divided

As they walked through the crowded high school reunion, their eyes met and they both froze. It had been over 50 years since they had last seen each other, yet the memories flooded back as if it were yesterday.

They sat down at a table in the corner and began to catch up. She had married her high school sweetheart and had three children. He had traveled the world, living life on his own terms, never settling down.

As they talked, they realized how different their lives had become. She had followed the path expected of her, while he had taken the road less traveled. He wondered if he had made the right choices in life, and she wondered if she had missed anything.

They both sat in silence for a moment, lost in thought. Then he spoke up, "Do you remember the poem we studied in English class? 'The Road Not Taken' by Robert Frost?"
She nodded, and he continued, "I always thought it was about choosing the adventurous path over the safe one. But now, looking back, I see that it's about the choices we make and the paths we take in life. We can never know what would have happened if we had taken a different path, but we can be grateful for the journey we have had."

She smiled and took his hand, "I always thought the poem was about taking risks and following your dreams, but now I see it's about being true to yourself and following your own path, even if it's not the popular one."

They sat together, lost in thought, thinking about the paths they had taken and the ones they could have taken. But for the moment, they were content with the paths that had led them to where they were now, together, rekindling an old flame and reminiscing about the past.

72 - Lost Hearts Unfound

Dr. Jameson has always been haunted by the memory of

the love letters he wrote to his high school sweetheart, Maria, and then burned in a fit of rage and despair. Now in his old age, he is a retired doctor with no family or friends to keep him company. He spends most of his days reading, watching television, and reminiscing about his past.

One day, while volunteering at the local hospice, he meets a terminally ill patient named Mrs. Johnson. She confides in him that she has a similar story to his, having burned the love letters she received from her late husband during a time of anger and grief. She wants to return the letters to her husband's family before she dies.

Moved by her story, Dr. Jameson decides to embark on a journey to find Maria and return the letters he wrote to her. With no current address or phone number, he begins by visiting her old high school, hoping to find a yearbook or alumni directory. Through sheer determination and a little luck, he finally tracks down Maria, now a retired schoolteacher living in a small town.

When they meet, Jameson is struck by how much she has changed since their youth. They spend a few hours catching up, reminiscing about their shared experiences and lost youth. Jameson finally gives Maria the letters he wrote all those years ago and apologizes for his past mistakes. Maria forgives him, and they both feel a sense of closure and peace.

As he drives home, Jameson reflects on the journey and the healing power of forgiveness. He realizes that it's never too late to make amends, and that life is too short to hold grudges and regrets. The experience inspires him to volunteer more at the hospice and to reach out to old friends and acquaintances. He begins to feel less lonely and more connected to the world around him.

73 - New Friends in Old Age

Once upon a time there was an elderly couple, Harold and Margaret. They had been married for over 50 years and had lived a long and happy life together. However, as they grew older, they began to experience some health problems and needed to move into an assisted living facility.

At first, Harold and Margaret were apprehensive about being away from their home and familiar surroundings. But they soon found themselves surrounded by a community of kind and caring people. They made friends with the other residents and staff and began to feel at home.

One day, Margaret was sitting in the garden enjoying the sunshine when she saw a young woman walking toward her. The woman had a small child with her, and they were carrying a basket of flowers.

"Excuse me," said the woman. "I noticed that you look like you could use some company, and my daughter and I would like to spend some time with you."

Margaret was touched by the woman's kindness and invited her and her daughter to sit with her in the garden. They talked for a while, and Margaret felt happy and content.

Over the next few weeks, the woman and her daughter visited Margaret and Harold regularly. They brought them flowers, books, and even some homemade treats. Harold was happy to have some company, too, and he and the little girl played cards together while Margaret and the woman chatted.

In time, Harold and Margaret's health improved and they were able to move back into their own home. But they never forgot the kindness of the woman and her daughter and kept in touch with them. They realized that no matter how old you are, there is always room in your heart for new friends.

Harold and Margaret's story reminds us that even in our later years, we can still find joy and happiness in the simple things, and that the kindness of strangers can make all the difference in the world.

74 - Elderly and Animals: A Heartwarming Bond

In a world that can often feel cold and disconnected, there is something truly heartwarming about the relationship between humans and animals. It is a connection that transcends age, race, and culture, bringing people together in ways that are both profound and beautiful.

For many older people, the companionship of animals is especially important. As we age, we may find ourselves living alone or facing health challenges that limit our ability to engage with the world around us. In these moments, the unconditional love and loyalty of a pet can make all the difference.

This is a truth that Rose, our protagonist, discovered for herself when she began volunteering at a local animal shelter. Despite her own age and limitations, she found that working with animals gave her a sense of purpose and meaning that she had not felt in years.

And it wasn't just Rose who benefited from the connection she made with the animals at the shelter. As she shared her love and affection with the cats, dogs and rabbits at the shelter, she found that her fellow volunteers and members of the community were drawn to her warmth and kindness.

But it was a little bunny named Buddy who stole Rose's heart. The frightened creature, sitting alone in the corner of the hutch, reminded her of her own vulnerability and need for connection. And in reaching out to Buddy, Rose found a source of joy and companionship that would bring her comfort for years to come.

Rose's story is a powerful example of how animals can enrich our lives and bring us together. And it is a reminder that even in our later years, we have the capacity to make meaningful connections and find joy in unexpected places.

75 - Nature's Uplifting Spirit

In today's fast-paced world, we often forget the magnificence and wonder of the natural world that surrounds us. Yet for some people, the beauty of nature is a source of comfort, motivation and happiness that can provide light in even the darkest of moments.

Margaret, a woman who cherished nature, had always found peace and inspiration in the natural world, from the towering trees of her childhood home to the delicate flowers in her garden. But it wasn't until a life-changing event that she truly realized the power of nature to heal and uplift.

After being diagnosed with cancer, Margaret struggled to find hope and meaning in her illness. But when she began exploring the woods and fields surrounding her home, she discovered a new sense of wonder and possibility that she had not felt in years.

As she watched the leaves turn from green to gold and felt the crisp autumn air on her skin, Margaret found herself reinvigorated with a sense of hope and determination. And as the seasons shifted and the natural world changed around her, she became stronger, more resilient, and more at peace with the difficulties she faced.

For Margaret, the beauty of nature was not just an escape from her troubles, but a reminder of the power of life and renewal. As she moved forward with her illness, she carried with her the knowledge that even in the darkest moments, there is always something beautiful and inspiring to be discovered in the natural world.
Margaret's story is a testament to the transformative power of nature in our lives. It reminds us that even in the face of adversity, the beauty and wonder of the natural world can provide us with hope and inspiration.

76 - Snowstorm Tales

The blizzard had been raging for days, and the seniors of the small town were trapped inside, unable to venture outside. But instead of feeling bored and restless, they found themselves gathered around the wood-burning fireplace in the local community center, sharing stories and memories of their past.
There was Mrs. Wilcox, who had been married for over fifty years, and Mr. Jenkins, who had never married but had his share of first loves and broken hearts. There was also Mrs. Bailey, who had lost her husband to cancer, and Mr. Lee, who had recently retired and felt lost without his job.
As they huddled around the fire, the seniors began to share their stories of love and heartbreak. Mrs. Wilcox told how she had met her husband, a young soldier, during World War II and how they had fallen in love despite the

uncertainty of the times. Mr. Jenkins talked about his first love, a girl he met in high school, and how he never forgot her, even after all these years.

Mrs. Bailey spoke of the pain of losing her husband and how she struggled to find meaning in life without him. And Mr. Lee shared his fear of growing old and losing his purpose now that he was no longer working.

As they talked, emotions ran high and secrets were revealed. Mrs. Wilcox admitted to having doubts about her marriage at times, and Mr. Jenkins confessed that his fear of rejection had kept him from pursuing love more often. Mrs. Bailey spoke of the guilt she felt for being alive while her husband was gone, and Mr. Lee shared his fear of dying alone.

Despite the heavy emotions, there was also a sense of renewal in the air. The seniors talked about the lessons they had learned from their past experiences and how they had become stronger and more resilient as a result. Mrs. Wilcox spoke about the importance of trust and communication in a marriage, and Mr. Jenkins spoke about the value of taking risks and pursuing love, even if it means risking rejection.

Mrs. Bailey talked about the power of community and support, and how the other seniors in the group helped her through her grief. And Mr. Lee spoke about the importance of finding new purpose and meaning in life, even after retirement.

As the blizzard continued outside, the seniors felt a sense of connection and camaraderie they had never experienced before. They talked late into the night, sipping warm tea and sharing memories of their past.

Eventually, the blizzard passed and the seniors were able to venture back outside. But the memories and lessons they had shared around the fireplace stayed with them, reminding them of the power of love, community, and renewal.

Their tales of first love, broken hearts, and renewal paralleled Jane Austen's Sense and Sensibility, the story of two sisters navigating the complexities of love and loss in the late 18th century. But unlike Austen's heroines, the seniors had already been through their own trials and tribulations and had emerged stronger and more resilient.

As they went about their daily lives, the seniors knew they would always have each other and the memories of their time together around the fireplace. And they also knew that they would continue to pursue love, adventure, and purpose, just as they had always done.

77 - Love Symphony

George and Margaret had been married for more than 60 years. They had shared a lifetime of memories, from raising their children to traveling the world together. But as they grew older, age-related health issues began to take their toll. Margaret's hearing had deteriorated, and George's speech had become slurred.

In spite of these challenges, George and Margaret remained deeply connected. They communicated through touch and gesture, and their love for each other grew stronger with each passing day.

One day, as George sat in his favorite chair, he began to hear a melody in his head. It was a simple melody, but it captured the essence of his love for Margaret in a way that words could no longer express.

Over the next few weeks, George continued to hear the melody in his head. He hummed it to himself as he went about his daily routine, and he began to realize that it was a symphony, a piece of music that represented the bond between him and Margaret.

Inspired by Richard Wagner's use of leitmotifs to represent characters and situations in his operas, George began to develop the symphony in his mind. Each movement represented a different aspect of their love, from the joys they shared in their early years to the challenges they faced in their later years.

As George worked on the symphony, he became more and more immersed in the music. It was as if he was channeling his love for Margaret into the notes, and with each passing day, the music grew more beautiful and complex.
When the symphony was finished, George knew it was time to share it with Margaret. He invited her to sit with him in the living room and began to play the symphony on the piano.
As the music filled the room, Margaret's face lit up with joy. She could feel the love and devotion that George had poured into the music, and she knew it was a tribute to their lifelong connection.

For the rest of the evening, George and Margaret listened to the symphony, lost in the beauty and complexity of the music. And though they could no longer communicate with words as they once had, they knew that their love was stronger than ever, and that it would continue to inspire them for the rest of their days.

In the weeks and months that followed, George continued to work on new pieces of music, each one inspired by his deep connection with Margaret. And even as her health continued to decline, they knew that their love was an inner symphony, a beautiful and complex expression of the bond they shared.

As George played the piano and Margaret listened, they knew that their love would continue to grow and blossom, even in the face of age and illness. For theirs was a love that transcended words, a love that could only be expressed through the beauty of music.

78 - Embracing the Present Moment with Family

As the family gathered for their annual reunion, Sarah sat quietly in a corner, watching her grandchildren and great-grandchildren play together. Her mind drifted back to happier times, to the days when she and her late partner, Jack, had taken trips to the beach and the mountains, explored the world together, and made memories that would last a lifetime.

But as the years passed, those memories had begun to fade. Sarah fought to hold on to them, to keep them alive in her mind, even as time seemed to slip away.

As she watched her family play, she felt a sense of longing, a yearning for the past, for the time when she and Jack had been young and full of life.

Drawing on Marcel Proust's Remembrance of Things Past, Sarah reflected on the ephemeral nature of existence, how memories and experiences could so easily slip away, leaving nothing but a faint trace of what once was.

But as she sat in that corner, watching her family play, she realized that there was something more lasting, more profound than mere memories. It was the intergenerational ties that bound them all together, the way her experiences paralleled those of her grandchildren and great-grandchildren, even as they played with their own toys and games.

For Sarah, the present was as important as the past, and she felt a sense of peace knowing that the memories she had shared with Jack were still alive in the experiences of her family, even if they were unaware of it.

As the day wore on, Sarah began to join in the activities, playing with her great-grandchildren and sharing stories of her youth. And as she laughed and played, she felt a sense of renewal, a rekindling of the joy and excitement she had once shared with Jack.

For even though the time lost could never be regained, Sarah knew that the time found in the present was just as precious, just as meaningful. And she realized that as long as her family continued to gather and play together, the memories of her past would continue to be reborn in the experiences of those she loved.

As the sun began to set and the family prepared to leave, Sarah felt a sense of contentment wash over her. She knew that the memories of her past would fade, but she also knew that they would live on in the experiences of those she loved.

For Sarah, the present was a time to cherish, a time to hold on to with all her heart. And she knew that as long as she was surrounded by the love and warmth of her family, the time lost could never truly be lost, for it would live on in the time found in the present moment.

79 - Reflections on Nature and Impermanence

Emily had always been fascinated by the natural world, finding solace in the ebb and flow of the seasons. Now retired and living alone, she took the opportunity to spend several months camping in a national park, immersing herself in the beauty of the wilderness.

As the spring sun began to rise over the forest, Emily sat by the fire, sipping her coffee and jotting observations in her journal. She noted the tender new growth of the trees, the sound of the birds singing their morning melodies, and the feel of the fresh mountain air on her skin.

As the weeks passed, Emily marveled at the transformation of the landscape. The leaves on the trees grew thicker and greener, and the wildflowers carpeted the ground in a rainbow of colors. Each day brought new discoveries, from the hatching of bird eggs to the emergence of insect larvae.

Emily found herself contemplating the impermanence of nature, the cycle of birth and death that played out all around her. She watched the leaves change color and fall from the trees, listened to the birds migrate south for the winter, and felt the chill of autumn creep into the air.

Despite the melancholy that came with these changes, Emily found comfort in the knowledge that nature would continue to evolve and renew itself. She wondered about her own impermanence and the inevitable cycle of life and death that awaited her. But for now, she enjoyed the beauty and tranquility of the natural world.

As winter approached, Emily packed up her campsite, leaving only her footprints. She returned home, eager to share her experiences with friends and family. But she also mourned the loss of the natural world she had come to love.

She wrote in her journal, "Nature is both constant and fleeting. It reminds us of the transience of our own lives and the importance of savoring every moment we have. I will always carry these memories with me as a reminder to appreciate the beauty of the world around us.

Emily's reflections echoed those of Samuel Taylor Coleridge, who famously wrote of the power of nature to connect us to our own mortality. As she read through her journal entries, Emily realized that her time in the wilderness had given her a new perspective on life and death and the ways in which they are intertwined.

For Emily, the natural world had become a source of comfort, a reminder that even as things change and pass, there is a constant cycle of renewal and rebirth. And as she faced an uncertain future, she knew she could always turn to nature for comfort and inspiration.

80 - Whimsical Musings

As the sun began to set, Mr. Brown and Mrs. Green met for their daily philosophical debate over tea. They were both retired professors who shared a passion for intellectual discourse. They sat at the garden table, surrounded by blooming flowers and chirping birds.
Mrs. Green took a sip of her tea and began, "I have been thinking about the concept of free will. Do we really have control over our actions, or is everything predetermined?"
Mr. Brown chuckled, "Ah, the age old debate. I believe we have some control, but the rest is fate."
Mrs. Green raised an eyebrow, "Interesting. But doesn't that imply a lack of responsibility for our actions?"
The debate went on for hours, covering topics such as religion, science, ethics, and the meaning of existence. Their conversations were always thought-provoking and stimulating.
As the days passed, they began to take long walks in the park, continuing their discussions on the way. They debated the latest scientific discoveries, shared their

opinions on the current political climate, and exchanged thoughts on the nature of love and friendship.

Their conversations were reminiscent of the academic discourse between J.R.R. Tolkien and C.S. Lewis, two brilliant minds who often met at the Eagle and Child pub in Oxford to discuss literature and philosophy.

Mr. Brown and Mrs. Green were both fascinated by the idea of life after death. Mrs. Green argued that consciousness could not exist without the physical brain, while Mr. Brown believed in the existence of a soul.
Their debates were never heated or argumentative, but rather respectful and thought-provoking. They challenged each other's beliefs and perspectives, always with an open mind and a thirst for knowledge.

As they sat at their garden table one day, Mr. Brown said, "I am grateful for our conversations, Mrs. Green. They bring a sense of purpose and fulfillment to my days.

Mrs. Green smiled warmly, "Me too, Mr. Brown. I feel that we're constantly learning from each other and broadening our perspectives."
Their conversations continued over the years, even as they aged and their health declined. They were both passionate about lifelong learning and the pursuit of knowledge.

They experienced a sense of comfort and contentment as they sat together amidst the beauty of nature and the simplicity of life. They knew that their conversations would continue to inspire and enlighten them as they entered the twilight years of their lives.

In the end, Mr. Brown and Mrs. Green's whimsical musings reminded them that intellectual curiosity and the pursuit of knowledge can bring a sense of purpose and fulfillment at any age.

81 - Rebuilding Hope

Once upon a time, there was a young woman named Samantha who dreamed of becoming a doctor. She was the first in her family to attend college and worked tirelessly to make her dream a reality. However, Samantha faced many challenges along the way, including financial struggles and personal setbacks.

Despite these obstacles, Samantha persevered and graduated from medical school with honors. She was proud to have achieved her goal and was ready to begin her career as a physician.

On her first day at the hospital, Samantha was nervous but excited. She met her colleagues and began seeing patients, eager to put her knowledge and skills into practice.
One day, a young boy was rushed to the hospital with a severe allergic reaction. Samantha and her team sprang into action, administering life-saving treatment and working together to stabilize the boy's condition.

As the boy's parents watched with tears in their eyes, Samantha felt a deep sense of accomplishment. She knew this was why she had become a doctor - to help people in their greatest time of need.

Over the next few months, Samantha continued to work hard, building relationships with her patients and colleagues. She faced challenges along the way, but she never lost sight of her passion for medicine and her desire to make a difference in people's lives.

One day, Samantha received a letter from a former patient thanking her for her care and compassion during a difficult time. Reading the letter brought tears to Samantha's eyes, knowing that her work had touched someone's life in a meaningful way.

From that day forward, Samantha continued to receive letters and messages from grateful patients and their families. And while she still faced challenges and long hours at the hospital, Samantha knew she was making a difference in the world and living her dream.

Looking back on her journey, Samantha realized that the challenges she had faced had only made her stronger and more determined. And she knew that if she could achieve her dream, anyone could - as long as they never gave up on their passions and never lost sight of their goals.

82 - The Unexpected Gift

Samantha had been depressed for weeks. She had lost her job, her relationship had ended, and she felt like she was going nowhere in life. She had been moping around her apartment for days, feeling sorry for herself, when she received a phone call from her best friend, Emily.

"Hey, Sam," Emily said. "I've got a surprise for you. I won a weekend at a fancy resort, but I can't go because of work. I thought you could use a change of scenery, so I'm giving it to you."
Samantha was taken aback. "Are you serious?" she asked. "That's amazing! But I can't accept such a big gift from you."
"Nonsense," Emily replied. "You need a break, and I want to help. Besides, it's non-refundable, so you might as well

use it."

Samantha felt a lump in her throat. She was overwhelmed by Emily's kindness and generosity. "Thank you so much," she said. "I don't know what to say."
"Just promise me you'll have a good time," Emily said. "You deserve it."

Samantha spent the next few days planning her trip. She packed her bags and drove to the resort, not knowing what to expect. When she arrived, she was overwhelmed by the beauty of the place. The sun was shining, the birds were singing, and the air was crisp and invigorating.

She spent the weekend exploring the resort, trying new foods and meeting new people. She took long walks, watched the sunset, and even tried yoga for the first time. For the first time in weeks, she felt truly alive.
As she packed her bags to go home, Samantha felt a sense of gratitude and appreciation wash over her. She realized that sometimes the best gifts in life are unexpected and come from the people who love us the most.

From that day on, Samantha made a promise to herself to focus on the good in her life, to appreciate the people who cared about her, and to pay it forward whenever she could. And she knew she had Emily to thank for showing her the way.

83 - Vintage Car Revival

The old car sat abandoned in the garage, covered in a thick layer of dust and cobwebs. It had been years since anyone had driven it, and many had assumed it was beyond repair. But to Max, the car represented a piece of history, a link to a simpler time when life moved at a slower pace.

As a young boy, Max had loved nothing more than sitting in the passenger seat of his father's old car and watching the world go by. He had learned to drive in that car, and had even taken it out for a spin on his first date. But as Max grew older and the car began to show its age, it had been retired to the garage, where it sat gathering dust.

But Max couldn't bear to see the car go to waste. He spent months rebuilding the engine, cleaning out the interior, and replacing the old tires. And finally, after countless hours of hard work, the car roared back to life.

Max was overjoyed. He took the car out for a spin, cruising the old country roads with the windows down and the wind in his hair. He felt a sense of freedom, a connection to the past he had missed for so long.

Soon Max found himself drawn to other old cars, scouring the Internet for listings and junkyards for parts. He spent his weekends at car shows and swap meets, talking with other enthusiasts and sharing stories of old times.

And as Max worked on his cars, he began to realize that the connection he felt to the past was more than just a love of old things. It was a deep appreciation for the craftsmanship and attention to detail that went into making these machines. It was a respect for the ingenuity and innovation that had shaped the world we live in.

Now, Max spends his weekends cruising the old country roads in his beloved old car, and he knows that as long as there are old cars to restore and stories to tell, he will always feel a connection to the past.

84 - The Power of a Simple Act of Kindness

Once upon a time, there was a young woman named Emily who had always dreamed of becoming a teacher. She worked hard in school and graduated with honors, but when she began applying for teaching jobs, she was met with rejection after rejection. It seemed that no one was interested in hiring a young, inexperienced teacher.

Feeling discouraged, Emily decided to take a break from her job search and volunteer at a local community center. There she met a group of children who quickly became her inspiration. They were bright, curious, and eager to learn, but many struggled with poverty, hunger, and neglect at home.

Emily decided to start a small tutoring program for the children at the center, offering help with homework, reading, and math. At first, only a few children showed up, but word spread and soon Emily had a full class of enthusiastic students.

Despite the challenges, Emily found joy in teaching and watching her students grow and learn. They came to trust and rely on her, not only for academic help, but also for emotional support and guidance.

One day, Emily received a call from a school district looking for a substitute teacher. She decided to give it a try and soon found herself in front of a classroom of rowdy middle schoolers. At first she was nervous, but then she remembered the lessons she had learned from her students at the community center: patience, kindness and a sense of humor.

To her surprise, the middle schoolers responded positively to her teaching style, and Emily soon found herself subbing more and more. Eventually, she was offered a full-time teaching position at a nearby school, which she happily accepted.

Years later, Emily looked back on her journey and realized that the rejection she had faced early on had been a blessing in disguise. It had led her to the community center and the students who had inspired her to become the kind of teacher she is today.

Now an experienced teacher with a classroom of her own, Emily has never forgotten the lessons she learned from her students at the community center: to be patient, to be kind, and to never give up on your dreams.

85 - A Second Chance

Emma has always been shy and introverted. She often felt uncomfortable in social situations and struggled to make friends. However, there was one thing that had always brought her joy and made her feel alive: singing.

Ever since she was a little girl, Emma loved to sing. She sang along to her favorite songs on the radio and dreamed of one day performing on stage in front of a large audience. But as she grew older, her shyness and self-doubt held her back. She never pursued her passion for singing and instead settled for a quiet life.

That all changed one day when Emma saw an ad for a local talent competition. It was called "Sing Your Heart Out," and it promised to give aspiring singers the chance to perform in front of a live audience and a panel of judges.

Emma felt a sudden surge of excitement and nervousness as she read the ad. Could this be her chance to finally pursue her dream of singing? She knew it would take a lot of courage to sign up, but something in her heart told her to do it.

With trembling hands, Emma filled out the application and

mailed it in. She spent the next few weeks practicing her favorite songs and trying to build her confidence.

Finally, the day of the competition arrived. Emma was a bundle of nerves as she walked onto the stage, but as soon as she started singing, all her fears melted away. She poured her heart and soul into the song, and when she finished, the crowd erupted in applause.

Emma couldn't believe it when she was announced as the winner of the competition. It was like a dream come true. For the first time in her life, she felt truly alive and confident.

From that day forward, Emma pursued her passion for singing with renewed vigor. She joined a local choir and began performing at open mic nights. She even began writing her own songs and recording them in a small studio.

Emma realized that it's never too late to pursue your dreams, and that sometimes all it takes is a little courage and a willingness to step outside your comfort zone. She was grateful for the talent competition that gave her the opportunity to finally find her voice and share it with the world.

86 - Adversity to Triumph

When Sarah was diagnosed with cancer, her world was turned upside down. She was only 30 years old, with two young children and a loving husband. The news was devastating, but Sarah refused to let it break her spirit.

With the support of her family and friends, Sarah began treatment. It was a long and difficult journey, filled with ups and downs. But Sarah was determined to fight, to do whatever it took to beat cancer and come out the other side stronger.

Throughout her treatment, Sarah turned to art as a way to cope. She had always enjoyed painting and drawing, but now it became a lifeline for her. She poured her emotions onto the canvas, creating beautiful works of art that captured the hope and resilience she felt deep inside.
As she painted, Sarah found a new sense of purpose. She realized that even in the darkest of times, there was beauty to be found. And as she shared her art with others, she saw the impact it had on their lives as well.

Sarah's cancer eventually went into remission, and she continued to create art as a way to express herself and inspire others. She even started a charity to provide art therapy to cancer patients and their families.
Looking back on her journey, Sarah realized that cancer had given her a gift. It had taught her to appreciate life in a new way, to find beauty in the everyday moments that once might have passed her by.

Today, Sarah's art continues to touch the lives of many. Her story is a reminder that even in the darkest of times, there is hope. And that sometimes the greatest gifts come from the most unexpected places.

87 - Memories of Youth

As we grow older, it's natural to reflect on the memories and experiences that have shaped us over the years. For many, these memories are a source of comfort and nostalgia, reminding us of a simpler time when life seemed simpler and full of possibilities.

One elderly couple in particular found themselves

transported back in time when they stumbled upon a box of old photographs from their youth. As they pored over each picture, memories flooded back and they found themselves reminiscing about a time when life was full of promise and excitement.

They recalled the adventures they had, the people they met, and the challenges they overcame, and with each story they felt a renewed sense of connection and purpose.

As they sat together, surrounded by the photographs of their youth, they were reminded of the resilience and strength that had carried them through so many difficult times. And as they looked to the future, they did so with a newfound sense of optimism and hope.

Their memories of the past had reminded them of the joy and fulfillment that comes from living a life of purpose and meaning, and they were determined to do so for as long as they could.

In the end, it's the memories of our youth that remind us of the beauty and potential that exists within each of us. They remind us of the people we once were, and the people we still have the capacity to become.

So as we grow older, let us remember the lessons of the past, and let us look to the future with a sense of optimism and hope. For it's the memories of the past that have the power to uplift and inspire us, and to remind us of the limitless potential that lies within each and every one of us.

88 - The Magic Garden

As a young girl, Emily had always loved spending time in

her grandfather's garden. He had a way with plants that seemed almost magical, drawing life from the soil in ways that left Emily spellbound.

Years passed, and Emily grew up and moved away, but her memories of her grandfather's garden remained as vivid as ever. So when she received the news that her grandfather had died, she knew the first place she had to go was to the garden.

As she walked among the rows of flowers and vegetables, memories flooded back and she found herself transported to those lazy afternoons spent chatting with her grandfather and watching him work his magic in the garden.
And then, as if by some kind of miracle, she noticed a single flower that seemed to glow with a warm, golden light. It was a flower she had never seen before, and yet it seemed somehow familiar, as if it had been waiting for her to come back and find it.

Emily couldn't explain it, but she felt a sense of peace and connection wash over her, as if her grandfather was somehow still with her, guiding her through the garden and showing her the beauty and wonder that exists all around us.

In that moment, she knew that her grandfather's legacy would live on, not only in the garden he had so lovingly tended, but in the memories and experiences he had shared with her throughout her life.
And as she left the garden, she carried with her a sense of gratitude and awe for the power of nature to connect us to our past and remind us of the beauty and wonder that still exists in the world around us.

89 - Forever Paws: A Story of Love

Sophie had always loved animals and dreamed of having a pet of her own since she was a little girl. Finally, when she was eight years old, her parents relented and let her adopt a stray kitten she had found wandering in the park.
Sophie named her new pet "Fluffy," and from that day on, the two were inseparable. Fluffy would curl up on Sophie's lap while she read or watched television, and they spent hours playing and exploring together.

As the years went by, Sophie grew up and moved away to college and then to a job in the city. But no matter where she went, Fluffy was always there, a constant source of comfort and companionship.

Then one day, Fluffy got sick. Sophie took her to the vet, but despite their best efforts, there was nothing they could do. Fluffy was gone.
Sophie was devastated, but as the days passed, she began to realize that Fluffy had left her with more than just memories. She had taught her about love and loyalty, and about the power of a simple purr or wag of the tail to brighten even the darkest day.

And so, in memory of Fluffy, Sophie began volunteering at a local animal shelter, helping to care for the animals there and find them new homes. She found that working with animals brought her a sense of peace and purpose that she had never known before, and she knew that Fluffy would be proud of the person she had become.
When she looked into the eyes of the animals she helped, Sophie felt a sense of connection and understanding that she knew only other pet owners could truly appreciate. And she knew deep down that no matter what life threw at her, she would always have the love and companionship of the pets she had come to cherish.

To Sophie, pets weren't just animals - they were family, and a source of joy and inspiration that would always be a part of her life.

90 - Pets and Purpose: Reflections on Life

Sophie had always loved animals and dreamed of having a pet of her own since she was a little girl. Finally, when she was eight years old, her parents relented and let her adopt a stray kitten she had found wandering in the park.
Sophie named her new pet "Fluffy," and from that day on, the two were inseparable. Fluffy would curl up on Sophie's lap while she read or watched television, and they spent hours playing and exploring together.

As the years went by, Sophie grew up and moved away to college and then to a job in the city. But no matter where she went, Fluffy was always there, a constant source of comfort and companionship.

Then one day, Fluffy got sick. Sophie took her to the vet, but despite their best efforts, there was nothing they could do. Fluffy was gone.
Sophie was devastated, but as the days passed, she began to realize that Fluffy had left her with more than just memories. She had taught her about love and loyalty, and about the power of a simple purr or wag of the tail to brighten even the darkest day.

And so, in memory of Fluffy, Sophie began volunteering at a local animal shelter, helping to care for the animals there and find them new homes. She found that working with animals brought her a sense of peace and purpose that she had never known before, and she knew that Fluffy would be proud of the person she had become.

When she looked into the eyes of the animals she helped, Sophie felt a sense of connection and understanding that she knew only other pet owners could truly appreciate. And she knew deep down that no matter what life threw at her, she would always have the love and companionship of the pets she had come to cherish.

To Sophie, pets weren't just animals - they were family, and a source of joy and inspiration that would always be a part of her life.

91 - Max, The Unexpected Joy in Mary's Life

As she sat in her favorite chair, surrounded by treasured family photos, Mary reflected on all the memories she had collected during her long life. At 95, she had lived through wars, economic downturns, and a world of change, but her spirit remained unbroken.

One day, while going through old photo albums, Mary came across a picture of herself as a young woman dancing with her husband at their wedding. The memory of that special day came flooding back and she felt a bittersweet pang of nostalgia. She missed her husband terribly, but she was also grateful for the life they had shared.

As Mary reminisced, she suddenly heard a knock at the door. It was her granddaughter, who had come to visit with a surprise. She had brought a rescue dog, a small terrier named Max, who was looking for a loving home.

At first, Mary was hesitant. She had never owned a pet before and was worried about the responsibility. But as soon as she held Max, she felt an instant connection. His wagging tail and wet nose brought a smile to her face and she knew she had found a new companion.

Over the next few weeks, Mary and Max bonded over long walks, games of fetch, and lazy afternoons cuddling on the couch. She loved the way he followed her around the house and how he always seemed to know when she needed a little extra love.

As Mary grew older, Max became her constant companion and source of joy. She often remarked to her family that she didn't know how she would have gotten through her later years without him. He had given her a renewed sense of purpose and a reason to get up each day.
And so, as Mary sat in her favorite chair, surrounded by the memories of a long and full life, she felt a sense of gratitude for the new memories she had created with Max. He had brought unexpected joy and companionship into her life, and she knew he would always have a special place in her heart.

92 - Unlikely Friendship: A Heartwarming Story

As the sun began to set on a warm summer evening, Olivia sat on her front porch and felt grateful for the simple pleasures in life. She had recently retired from her job as a nurse and was enjoying her newfound freedom. But something was missing. Although she had a close-knit family and a few close friends, Olivia often felt lonely.
One day, while walking in the park, Olivia came across a group of children playing together. She couldn't help but smile at their carefree laughter and energy. As she watched them, she felt a tug at her heartstrings. She realized she missed the joy and innocence of childhood.
The next day, Olivia decided to volunteer at a local after-school program for underprivileged children. As soon as

she walked in the door, the children greeted her with hugs and smiles. She was struck by their resilience and ability to find happiness in the face of adversity.

Over the next few weeks, Olivia became a regular volunteer at the program. She helped with homework, played games and listened to the children's stories. As she got to know them, she realized that they had given her something she was missing: a sense of purpose.

One day, one of the children asked Olivia why she volunteered. She paused for a moment, trying to think of an answer. Finally, she said, "Because you make me happy. Seeing your smiles and hearing your laughter brings me joy. And I hope that in some small way I can make your lives a little better.

The children's faces lit up, and Olivia knew she had made a difference. From that moment on, she realized she had found a new purpose in life. She continued to volunteer with the program, and the children became her extended family.

As Olivia sat on her front porch and watched the sun sink below the horizon, she felt a sense of fulfillment. She realized that it wasn't just the children who had benefited from her volunteer work; she had gained so much from the experience as well. She had found new meaning in her life and discovered that sometimes the smallest acts of kindness can have the greatest impact.

93 - A Little Girl's Act of Kindness

As a newborn, John was abandoned in a hospital with no family to call his own. He was taken in by the staff and placed in foster care, where he bounced from home to home, never quite finding the love and stability he craved.

As the years passed, John grew into a troubled teenager. He struggled with addiction, anger, and a sense of hopelessness. But despite his struggles, he never lost the spark of resilience that had kept him going all these years.

One day, John met a woman named Sarah. She volunteered at a local shelter and had a passion for helping young people in need. She saw something special in John, a glimmer of potential that others had overlooked.
Sarah took John under her wing and became his mentor. She helped him get the support and resources he needed to overcome his addiction and turn his life around. With her guidance, John found a sense of purpose and direction he had never known before.

As John worked toward his goals, Sarah became like family to him. She was there to celebrate his victories and support him through his setbacks. She showed him that he was worthy of love and belonging, and that he had a bright future ahead of him.

Years later, John stood at the altar waiting for his bride to walk down the aisle. As he looked out at the crowd, he saw Sarah smiling at him from the front row. She had been his rock and his inspiration, and he knew he wouldn't be standing here today without her. After the ceremony, John walked over to Sarah and hugged her. "Thank you," he said. "For everything." Sarah smiled and squeezed his hand. "You did all the hard work, John. I just helped guide you to your true potential."

As John and his new wife began their life together, he knew he would never forget the kindness and support Sarah had given him. She had shown him that with a little love and encouragement, anything was possible.

94 - A Little Kindness Goes a Long Way

Samantha was always a kind and caring person. She believed in the power of small acts of kindness and went out of her way to help those in need. So when she heard about a local charity that was struggling to keep up with demand, she knew she had to do something.

Samantha decided to volunteer her time and skills to the charity and soon became a regular volunteer at their events. She loved the feeling of making a difference in people's lives, no matter how small. Whether it was serving food at a homeless shelter or organizing a fundraiser, Samantha felt fulfilled knowing she was doing good.

Then one day, Samantha received a letter in the mail. It was from a woman named Maria who had attended one of the charity events Samantha had helped with. Maria wrote about how much the event had meant to her and how grateful she was for the kindness of Samantha and the other volunteers.

As Samantha read the letter, she was overcome with emotion. She realized that even the smallest acts of kindness can have a profound impact on someone's life. She was grateful to be able to make a difference and vowed to continue to do so as long as she could.

Over the years, Samantha continued to volunteer with the organization and inspired others to do the same. Her kindness and generosity touched countless lives, and she became known in her community as a beacon of hope and positivity.

Ultimately, Samantha realized that the meaning of life is not about achieving personal success or accumulating wealth, but about making a positive impact on the world.

She felt grateful for the opportunity to serve others and knew that her small acts of kindness had made a big difference in the lives of many.

95 - A Honeymoon to Remember

As soon as they said "I do," Jack and Emily knew they were meant to be together forever. They had been planning their honeymoon for months, dreaming of white sandy beaches, clear blue waters, and lazy afternoons spent basking in the sun.

When they finally arrived at their destination, they were in awe of the natural beauty that surrounded them. They spent their days snorkeling, hiking, and exploring the island, and their nights dancing under the stars.
As their honeymoon drew to a close, Jack and Emily realized that their trip had been much more than just relaxation and adventure. It had been a time for them to truly connect with each other and strengthen their love.
As they boarded the plane to return home, they knew they were embarking on a new journey together. Life would bring challenges and obstacles, but they were confident they could face anything as long as they were together.

As the years passed, Jack and Emily remained as happy as ever. They had built a life filled with love, laughter, and adventure. Then one day, Emily was diagnosed with a serious illness. The news was devastating, and Jack felt like his world was falling apart.
But as they faced this new challenge together, they drew strength from memories of their honeymoon. They remembered how they had felt so connected and in love, and knew they could face this challenge as a team.

Emily underwent treatments and surgeries, and although it was a difficult time, Jack was by her side every step of the way. And when she finally went into remission, they knew they had come through this challenge stronger than ever.

Looking back on their honeymoon, they realized that it had been more than just a vacation. It had been a foundation for their love, a reminder of the deep connection they shared. And as they looked forward to their future, they knew that as long as they were together, they could face anything.

96 - A Story of Old Times

As she walked through the park, Sarah couldn't help but think about the old days. She had lived a long and full life, but there was something special about reminiscing about her youth.

She sat down on a bench and closed her eyes, transported back to a time when life was simpler and full of promise. She remembered the summer days spent playing with her friends, the nights spent dancing to jazz music, and the feeling of falling in love for the first time.
As she sat there, lost in thought, she felt a tap on her shoulder. It was a young couple, holding hands and smiling. They had noticed her daydreaming and asked if they could join her. Sarah welcomed the company and began to tell stories of her youth.
She spoke of the war and the hardships it brought, but also

of the moments of hope and camaraderie that kept her going. She spoke of her late husband and the life they had built together, full of love and adventure.

As she spoke, Sarah realized that although the world had changed so much, the human experience remained the same. Love, friendship, and hope were constants, and the memories of her youth were still cherished and precious.

The young couple listened intently, captivated by Sarah's stories and wisdom. As they said their goodbyes, they thanked her for reminding them that life is full of precious moments to be cherished.

Sarah sat for a while, watching the world go by and feeling grateful for the memories she had collected during her long life. She realized that even though time had passed, the joy and meaning she had found in the old times would always be a part of her.

97 - The Gift of Time

As a child, Emily loved spending time with her grandfather. They would sit on the porch swing and talk for hours, sharing stories and enjoying each other's company. But as Emily grew older and life got busier, she found herself visiting less and less.

Then one day she received a phone call from her mother. Her grandfather had fallen ill and was not expected to recover. Emily was devastated at the thought of losing him and realized that she had taken his presence for granted.

When she arrived at her grandparents' house, Emily was struck by how frail and weak her grandfather looked. He smiled weakly as she sat by his bedside, and she felt a pang of regret for not visiting more often.

As the days passed, Emily spent as much time as she could with her grandfather, holding his hand and reminiscing about old times. She listened as he told stories of his youth and the lessons he had learned over the years. She realized how much wisdom he had to offer and how much she had missed by not making time for him.

One day, as Emily sat with her grandfather, he reached into his nightstand and pulled out an old pocket watch. He handed it to her and said, "I want you to have this. It's been in our family for generations, and I want you to remember how important it is to take time for the people you love.
Emily was touched by the gift and the sentiment behind it. She realized that time was the most precious gift of all, and that she needed to make a conscious effort to prioritize the people who mattered most to her.

Emily kept the pocket watch with her after her grandfather died to remind her of the gift of time and the importance of taking care of our loved ones. She vowed to never take anyone for granted and to always make time for her loved ones.

98 - A New Perspective

Once upon a time, there was a young man named Adam who had recently graduated from college. He had always dreamed of starting his own business, but he didn't know where to start.
One day, in his grandfather's attic, he came across an old book that belonged to his great-great-grandfather, who had been a successful entrepreneur. The book was filled with wisdom and advice about starting and running a

business.

As Adam read the book, he felt a spark of inspiration. He decided to follow in his ancestor's footsteps and start his own business. Using the advice in the book and his own hard work, he was able to build a successful business.

Years later, when Adam looked through the old book again, he found a note tucked inside. It was a letter from his great-great-grandfather to his future descendants. In the letter, he wrote about the challenges he faced in starting his own business, but also about the incredible sense of fulfillment and pride he felt in creating something of his own.

After reading the letter, Adam felt a deep connection to his ancestor and the legacy he left behind. He realized that the book and letter were not just about business, but about the importance of following your dreams and creating a life you can be proud of.

With renewed inspiration, Adam continued to grow his business and mentor others just starting out. He knew that his great-great-grandfather would be proud of him and that his own legacy would continue for generations to come.

This story reminds us that sometimes the greatest inspiration and guidance can come from the wisdom of our ancestors. We can learn from their experiences and use their teachings to create a better future for ourselves and those around us.

99 - Innovative Minds: Greatest Inventions

Necessity is the mother of invention. Throughout history, people have faced challenges and problems that required innovative solutions. From the wheel to the telephone, these inventions have changed the way we live, work and communicate.

One such invention that had a profound impact on the world was the printing press. Before Johannes Gutenberg invented the printing press in the 15th century, books were copied by hand, making them expensive and rare. The printing press allowed for the mass production of books, making them more accessible and affordable to the masses.

Another famous invention is the light bulb, which was invented by Thomas Edison in 1879. Edison conducted countless experiments to find a material that would work as a filament in the bulb, finally settling on charred bamboo. The light bulb revolutionized the world, allowing people to work and live beyond the hours of daylight and ushering in a new era of technological advancement.

But sometimes inventions come from unexpected places. In the 20th century, a woman named Grace Hopper invented the compiler, a program that translates written code into machine-readable language. Hopper was a pioneer in computer programming, and her work laid the foundation for modern computer software.

These inventions are just a few examples of how human ingenuity can shape the course of history. They show us that even in the face of seemingly insurmountable challenges, we have the power to create solutions that can change the world for the better.

So the next time you turn on a light switch or read a book, take a moment to appreciate the inventors who made these things possible. They were ordinary people who saw a need and had the courage to pursue their ideas, no matter how unconventional they may have seemed at the time.

Their legacy lives on in the world-changing inventions that continue to make our lives easier, more fulfilling, and more connected. And who knows? The next great invention may be just around the corner, waiting for someone with the vision and determination to bring it to life.

100 - Journey of the Heart: Finding Joy in Travel

As a young woman, Emily always dreamed of traveling the world. She longed to see new sights, taste exotic foods, and immerse herself in different cultures. But as she grew older, life got in the way and her dream seemed more and more out of reach.

One day, at the age of 55, Emily decided that enough was enough. She made a list of all the places she had always wanted to visit and began planning her first trip. She didn't know how many more opportunities she would have, so she was determined to make the most of every moment.

Her first destination was Paris. The romance and beauty of the city had always captivated her, and it did not disappoint. She spent her days wandering the streets, admiring the architecture, and enjoying croissants and coffee at outdoor cafés. At night, she attended shows at the Moulin Rouge and danced under the stars in Montmartre.

Next on Emily's list was Japan. She was fascinated by the ancient culture, breathtaking gardens and vibrant street life. She spent a week in Tokyo, exploring temples, trying new foods, and soaking up the neon lights of Shibuya. She then traveled to Kyoto, where she visited the geisha district and participated in a traditional tea ceremony.

Over the next few years, Emily continued to check destinations off her list. She visited the beaches of Bali, the ruins of Machu Picchu, and the colorful streets of Marrakech. Each trip was an adventure, and she treasured every experience, big and small.

As Emily looked back on her travels, she realized that they had given her something she had long been missing: a sense of wonder and excitement. She felt alive and vibrant in a way she hadn't in years. She was grateful for the memories she had made and the new friends she had made along the way.

Now in her seventies, Emily continues to travel whenever she can. She knows there is still so much to see and experience in this beautiful world, and she looks forward to whatever adventures lie ahead.

101 - Finding Happiness: A Meadowville Story

In the small town of Meadowville, nestled among rolling hills and colorful meadows, lived a woman named Emily. Despite facing many challenges in life, she always had a bright smile on her face and a genuine kindness that touched everyone she met. People were drawn to her positive energy and unwavering optimism.

Emily had a unique perspective on happiness. She believed that true happiness came not from external circumstances, but from within. She understood that happiness was a choice - one that could be made even in the face of adversity. And so, every day, she made a conscious decision to embrace the joy that life had to offer.

One summer day, as Emily walked through the town

square, she noticed a young boy sitting alone on a bench, his face filled with sadness. Curious, she approached him and struck up a conversation. The boy, named Jack, had recently lost his beloved dog and was struggling to find happiness again.

Emily listened intently to Jack's story and shared her own experiences of loss and finding happiness in the midst of the darkest moments. She spoke of the power of gratitude, of cherishing memories, and of finding solace in the simple pleasures of life. As they talked, Emily's words resonated deeply with Jack, and a spark of hope began to flicker within him.

In the weeks that followed, Emily became a guiding light in Jack's life. She introduced him to the beauty of nature, taking him on walks through the meadows and teaching him to appreciate the smallest wonders - like the vibrant colors of a butterfly or the melodious songs of birds. She showed him that happiness can be found in the simplest of moments, if only one looks with open eyes and a grateful heart.

Over time, Jack's sadness slowly gave way to a newfound sense of joy. He began to see the world through Emily's eyes, embracing each day with renewed enthusiasm. Their friendship grew stronger, and the townspeople marveled at the positive change they saw in Jack.

Word of Emily's extraordinary ability to inspire happiness spread throughout the town, and soon people sought her out for guidance. She organized community events that brought people together to share stories, laughter, and acts of kindness. Through her unwavering belief in the power of happiness, Emily touched the lives of countless people, reminding them that happiness is a gift we can give ourselves and others.

Emily's legacy lives on in Meadowville, where her teachings have become part of the fabric of the town. Her unwavering spirit serves as a reminder that happiness is not simply a destination, but a lifelong journey-one that begins with a choice and flourishes through love, gratitude, and the beauty found in each precious moment.

102 - A Love Woven in Time

In the quiet corners of an old farmhouse, where time had left its gentle mark on the weathered walls, lived an elderly couple named Harold and Eleanor. Their days were filled with memories of times past, when life seemed simpler and hearts beat in unison with the rhythms of nature.

As dusk cast its golden glow over the world, Harold and Eleanor would gather by the fireplace, their hearts woven with the threads of nostalgia. With eager anticipation, they would delve into their treasure trove of photographs, letters, and memorabilia, stepping back into the tapestry of their shared history.

One evening, while rummaging through a dusty box, Eleanor's eyes sparkled with delight as she stumbled upon an old journal, its pages yellowed with age. It was Harold's diary from their youth, a time when dreams were etched on the canvas of their souls.

Their curiosity piqued, they began to read aloud the journal's delicate words, weaving a tale of their early encounters, stolen glances, and whispered promises. The diary took them back to a world where love blossomed under starry skies, where their hearts danced to a symphony of youthful passion.

With each turn of the page, laughter filled the room as they relived the mischievous adventures and cherished memories they had created together. The stories unfolded like a delicate tapestry, each thread connecting them to a time of innocence and wonder.

As the night wore on, the flame of their love burned brighter and brighter. They marveled at how their bond had weathered life's storms, growing stronger with each trial and tribulation. Their shared laughter, tears, and moments of quiet understanding had forged an unbreakable bond, like the ancient oaks that stood tall outside their window.

With overflowing hearts, Harold and Eleanor realized that the power of their love had transcended time. Their memories were not relics of the past, but living echoes resonating in their present. Their love story, written in the pages of this weathered journal, had become a testament to the enduring power of the human spirit.

And so, nestled in the embrace of the past, Harold and Eleanor found solace and joy. They discovered that the past was not meant to be left behind, but to be cherished, celebrated, and passed on to the next generation. Their love story became a guiding light, reminding them and others that true love, like their memories, is timeless, eternal, and forever alive in their hearts.

103 - The Gift of Connection

In a bustling city where people hurried past each other without a second glance, there lived an elderly woman named Margaret. She had spent most of her days alone, her only company the memories of a lifetime. Little did she know that a chance encounter would bring a beautiful change to her world.

One chilly afternoon, as Margaret strolled through the park, she noticed a little girl sitting on a bench with tears streaming down her face. Concerned, Margaret approached her and asked what was wrong. The girl, named Emily, explained that she had been separated from her parents and did not know how to find them.

Moved by Emily's distress, Margaret decided to help. She held Emily's hand and assured her that everything would be okay. Together, they embarked on a mission to reunite Emily with her family. Margaret's heart warmed as she saw the trust and hope in the young girl's eyes.
As they searched the park, Margaret couldn't help but share snippets of her own life. She told Emily of old times, of dances under starry skies and picnics in sun-kissed meadows. Margaret's stories brought a sparkle to Emily's eyes and eased her worries.

After what seemed like an eternity, they finally spotted Emily's parents, who were anxiously searching for her. Margaret's heart swelled with joy as she witnessed the tearful reunion. Emily's parents were so grateful for Margaret's help that they invited her to join them for a cup of tea.
That day marked the beginning of a remarkable bond between Margaret and Emily's family. They discovered that their lives had been intertwined for a reason. Margaret became a treasured part of Emily's life, and Emily brought laughter and youthful energy back into Margaret's world.

Together, they created new memories - afternoons filled with laughter, baking cookies, and sharing stories. Margaret no longer felt alone, for she had found family in Emily and her parents.

In the gift of connection, Margaret discovered that love and friendship know no age limits. As they embraced the beauty of their shared moments, they realized that sometimes the most meaningful relationships are found when we least expect them.

And so Margaret and Emily's family embarked on a journey of love, teaching each other the timeless lesson that true companionship can be found in the unlikeliest of places.

104 - Embracing the Power of Compassion

In a small town nestled among rolling hills, there lived a woman named Grace. Her warm smile and gentle spirit touched the lives of everyone she met. Despite her own struggles, she found solace in helping others and spreading love.

One fateful day, Grace met a young man named David. David had lost his job and was struggling financially. Despair weighed heavily on his heart as he wondered how he would provide for his family. Seeing his anguish, Grace's compassionate heart reached out to him.

Grace offered David a listening ear and a comforting presence. She knew that sometimes all someone needed was to know they were not alone. Through their conversations, Grace learned of David's passion for woodworking, a skill he had developed in happier times. Inspired by his talent, Grace had an idea.

With the support of the community, Grace organized a small craft fair in the town square. The event showcased local artisans, and Grace invited David to display his woodworking creations. David was hesitant at first, unsure if anyone would be interested in his work. But Grace's unwavering belief in him gave him the courage to participate.

On the day of the fair, the town gathered, curious to see the talent on display. To David's surprise, his handmade wooden pieces captivated the crowd. People marveled at his craftsmanship and the love he put into each creation. Before long, his creations sold out, leaving David overwhelmed with gratitude.

The success of the craft fair inspired David to pursue his passion. He began receiving custom orders and gaining recognition as a skilled artisan. Through it all, Grace stood by his side, offering guidance and encouragement.

In time, David's financial situation improved and he found stability for his family. But the true gift he received was not just financial security-it was a belief in himself and a reminder that kindness has the power to change lives.

Grace's act of kindness had a ripple effect, inspiring others in the community to reach out and support those in need. Her selfless actions set off a chain reaction of compassion, reminding everyone that even the smallest acts of kindness can make a world of difference.

In the heartwarming embrace of Grace's kindness, David learned that sometimes the greatest blessings come from the hands and hearts of strangers. And he vowed to carry that spirit of generosity with him, knowing it has the power to heal and uplift the souls of all who cross his path.

105 - A Heartwarming Tale from World War II

In the midst of the chaos and darkness that consumed the world during World War II, there was a small glimmer of light that shone brightly in the hearts of two strangers, Robert and Emma.

Robert, a young soldier fighting on the front lines, longed

for the warmth and comfort of home. He carried a photograph of his beloved family, a reminder of the love that fueled his determination to survive the horrors of war. Amid the relentless fighting, he found solace in the handwritten letters he received from strangers who offered words of encouragement and support.

Emma, a compassionate nurse, dedicated herself to caring for the wounded and weary. She witnessed firsthand the devastating toll that war takes on the human spirit. But she refused to be overcome by despair. Instead, she channeled her energy into acts of kindness and compassion, bringing comfort to those who needed it most.
Fate brought Robert and Emma together at a moment of despair and uncertainty. In a field hospital, Robert lay wounded, his mind flickering as he struggled with the physical and emotional wounds of war. Emma tended to his injuries with her gentle touch and unwavering compassion, and lifted his spirits with her soothing words.

Their bond grew stronger with each passing day. They shared stories of hope, dreams of a better future, and found solace in the presence of someone who understood the weight they carried on their shoulders. Their bond transcended the boundaries of war, offering them a glimmer of hope in the midst of darkness.

As the war raged on, Robert and Emma found strength in each other. Their love became a beacon of light that guided them through the darkest of times. They reminded each other of the power of kindness, compassion, and the indomitable human spirit.

Years later, their love story continues to inspire and touch the hearts of those who hear it. It serves as a reminder that even in the face of adversity, love and compassion can triumph. Robert and Emma's story echoes through the annals of history, reminding us of the enduring power of the human heart.

106 - A Bond Beyond Blood: A Tale of Adoption

In a small town nestled in the countryside, a couple named Sarah and David longed for a child to call their own. Their hearts brimmed with love and they were eager to share their lives with a little one. Despite their own challenges, they believed in the power of family and were determined to make their dream come true through adoption.

Months turned into years as they navigated the emotional roller coaster of paperwork, interviews, and waiting. Doubts and fears crept into their minds, but their unwavering faith in the journey kept them going. They immersed themselves in books about parenting, attended support groups, and connected with other hopeful parents. Their resilience and determination were fueled by the unwavering belief that their child was out there, waiting to join their loving embrace.

Finally, the long-awaited call came. A bright-eyed baby girl named Lily had entered their lives. From the moment they held her in their arms, their souls intertwined and a bond of unconditional love formed. Sarah and David discovered that biology did not define their family; it was the love they shared that made them whole.

As the years passed, Sarah and David marveled at the beauty of parenthood. They watched Lily grow, blossom, and pursue her dreams with unbridled passion. Each milestone was celebrated with joy and gratitude, for they understood the precious gift they had been given. Through life's ups and downs, they stood by Lily's side, providing unwavering support, guidance, and love.

In the heartwarming story of Sarah, David, and Lily, we find the power of family and the profound impact of adoption. It is a story that celebrates the resilience of the human spirit and the unbreakable bond that forms when hearts open to love. Sarah and David's journey reminds us that the road to parenthood is not always straight, but the destination is filled with immeasurable joy and the transformative power of unconditional love.

This inspiring story of child adoption invites us to reflect on the incredible gift of family and the profound impact a loving home can have on a child's life. It reminds us that love knows no boundaries and that every child deserves a place to call home, filled with love, support and endless possibilities.

107 - A Heartwarming Tale of Success

In a bustling city where towering skyscrapers rose above crowded streets, there lived a young girl named Lily. Growing up in a modest neighborhood, she knew all too well the harsh realities of poverty. Her parents worked tirelessly, struggling to make ends meet and provide for their family.

Despite the challenges they faced, Lily's parents instilled in her the belief that education was the key to a brighter future. With their unwavering support and encouragement, Lily pursued her studies with burning determination.
Her school was a sanctuary where her dreams took flight. Lily's hunger for knowledge was insatiable, and she immersed herself in books and learning. Her teachers saw her potential and nurtured her talents, providing guidance and mentorship.

As Lily grew older, she faced moments of doubt and uncertainty. The weight of poverty threatened to crush her dreams, but she refused to let it define her. With unwavering resilience, she embraced each setback as an opportunity for growth and pushed herself to work harder.

Lily's perseverance paid off when she won a scholarship to a prestigious university. It was a turning point in her life, a chance to break out of the cycle of poverty that had gripped her family for generations. With every lecture, every assignment, Lily soaked up knowledge like a sponge, determined to create a better life for herself and her loved ones.

Graduation day arrived, and Lily stood on the stage in cap and gown, her heart overflowing with pride and gratitude. Her parents, tears streaming down their faces, witnessed their daughter's remarkable journey. The applause echoed throughout the auditorium, a resounding testament to Lily's strength and determination.

In the years that followed, Lily went on to achieve great success. She became a prominent figure in her field, using her influence to uplift others from similar backgrounds. Through her philanthropic efforts, she provided scholarships and opportunities to children facing poverty, giving them the chance to rewrite their own stories.

Lily's journey serves as a beacon of hope, a testament to the power of resilience and hard work. Her story reminds us that success knows no boundaries and that even in the face of adversity, we have the strength to overcome and create a better future.

108 - Embracing Joy: A Heartwarming Journey

There was a small girl named Lily who had a special viewpoint on happiness in a crowded city full of rushed footsteps and busy life. Lily found happiness in the most basic things, whereas others were obsessed by the desire of achievement and worldly goods.

One sunny afternoon, as Lily walked through a park, she noticed an elderly man sitting on a bench with a gentle smile on his face. Intrigued, she approached him and asked, "Sir, what makes you so happy?"
The man chuckled and patted the empty seat on the bench beside him, inviting Lily to sit down. He shared his wisdom, explaining that happiness is not found in external circumstances, but in the way we choose to perceive the world around us.
He told Lily about his own journey, how he had once chased after wealth and status, only to realize that true happiness lay in the moments of connection and appreciation for life's simple pleasures.

Together they watched children playing in a nearby playground, their laughter filling the air. The man pointed out the joy and innocence in their faces, reminding Lily that happiness can be found in the purest and most genuine expressions of joy.

As their conversation continued, Lily opened her heart to the man's words of wisdom. She learned that happiness can be found in a warm hug, a kind word, or a shared laugh. It can be found in the beauty of nature, the taste of a favorite treat, or the comfort of a familiar song.

Inspired by the man's perspective, Lily began to see the world with new eyes. She discovered happiness in the vibrant colors of a sunset, the sound of raindrops on her window, and the embrace of loved ones.

From that day forward, Lily carried the older man's wisdom with her and embraced the small moments that brought happiness into her life. She learned that happiness is not a destination to be reached, but a choice to be made each day.
And so, with a heart full of gratitude and a newfound appreciation for life's simple joys, Lily embarked on a journey of true happiness, spreading warmth and smiles wherever she went.

109 - Heartwarming Philanthropy Stories

Once upon a time, in a small town nestled among rolling hills, there lived a remarkable woman named Sarah. Her heart overflowed with compassion, and she dedicated her life to making a difference in the lives of others. Despite limited resources, Sarah believed in the power of philanthropy and the impact it could have on her community.

Every day, Sarah woke up with a sense of purpose, eager to spread joy and bring hope to those in need. She began by organizing food drives and reaching out to local businesses and individuals to collect donations. With unwavering determination, she ensured that no one in her town would go hungry. The smiles on the faces of those who received the food baskets were priceless, and Sarah's heart swelled with joy.

But Sarah's philanthropic spirit didn't stop there. Recognizing that education is a powerful tool for change, she set out to provide scholarships to deserving students who couldn't afford to pursue their dreams. Sarah's tireless efforts and unwavering belief in the potential of these young minds opened doors that once seemed closed. Each success story became a testament to the transformative power of her philanthropy.

As word of Sarah's selfless acts spread, more people were inspired to join her cause. Together, they organized fundraisers, volunteered their time and contributed their resources to support Sarah's mission. The ripple effect of their kindness reached far beyond the city, touching lives and igniting a spirit of giving in others.

Through her journey, Sarah discovered that philanthropy isn't just about giving material things. It was about touching hearts, restoring hope, and fostering a sense of community. She witnessed firsthand the incredible impact each act of kindness has on both the giver and the receiver.

Sarah's story reminds us that we all have the power to make a difference, no matter our circumstances. Philanthropy isn't limited to grand gestures; it can be as simple as lending a listening ear, offering a helping hand, or spreading kindness wherever we go.

So let us be inspired by Sarah's unwavering dedication and embrace the spirit of philanthropy in our own lives. Together, we can create a world where compassion and generosity thrive and the true meaning of humanity shines brightly.

110 - Gratitude's Radiance

In a world where busyness often consumes our lives, there

lived a woman named Grace. She had a unique perspective that set her apart - a heart filled with gratitude that radiated warmth and touched the lives of those around her.

Grace awoke each morning with a grateful heart, eager to embrace the blessings of the day. As she sipped her morning coffee, she marveled at the aroma and savored each sip, appreciating the simple pleasures that brought joy to her life.

One day, while waiting in line at the grocery store, Grace noticed an elderly man struggling to reach an item on the top shelf. Without hesitation, she stepped forward and offered to help. The man's face lit up with gratitude, and in that moment, a beautiful connection was made.

Inspired by this encounter, Grace embarked on a gratitude journey, looking for ways to express appreciation and kindness. She wrote heartfelt thank-you notes to her loved ones, took time to listen to friends in need, and volunteered at local charities, sharing her time and resources.

As Grace continued her journey, she discovered that gratitude has the power to transform not only her own life, but the lives of others as well. The simple act of saying "thank you" had the ability to brighten someone's day, mend broken spirits, and create lasting connections.

One winter evening, Grace organized a gathering at her community center and invited people from all walks of life to share their stories of gratitude. The room buzzed with laughter and tears of joy as each person expressed heartfelt appreciation for the blessings in their lives.

As the evening drew to a close, Grace looked around the room, filled with gratitude for the connections she had made and the love that had been shared. She realized that gratitude is a gift that multiplies when shared, enriching the lives of both giver and receiver.

From that day forward, Grace continued to cultivate gratitude in her life and inspire others to do the same. Through her unwavering appreciation, she created a ripple effect of kindness, compassion, and joy in her community.

In a world that often focuses on what is lacking, Grace reminded everyone that gratitude is the key to unlocking a life of abundance. Her story served as a gentle reminder that there is something to be grateful for in every moment- a spark of light that illuminates even the darkest of days.

ABOUT THE AUTHOR

Susanne B. Flores is a passionate writer and author of the heart-warming book "110 Uplifting Short Stories for the Elderly". With a background in gerontology and a deep love for storytelling, she creates inspiring narratives that touch the hearts of readers of all ages. Her work aims to bring joy and hope to seniors and their families.

Your Free Gift

As a way of saying thanks for your purchase, I've also put together your gift to download now online: A relaxing **background track** to help you enjoy your reading time.

www.learning-adventures-press.com/download

Leave a review

As an independent author with a small marketing budget, reviews are my livelihood on this platform. If you enjoyed this book, I'd really appreciate it if you leave your honest feedback. I love hearing from my readers, and I personally read every review.

Thank you, Susanne B. Flores

Made in United States
Troutdale, OR
07/24/2023

11521458R00091